THE THREAD THAT BINDS US

GILLIAN ROTHWELL ROSE

Copyright ©2019 Gillian Rothwell Rose

Author: Gillian Rothwell Rose

The Thread That Binds Us / Gillian Rothwell Rose

ISBN: 9781652228837

Book Cover: Wallgate, Wigan, England.

All rights reserved, which includes the right to reproduce this book or portions thereof in any form whatsoever except as provided by the U.S. Copyright Law.

PRINTED IN THE UNITED STATES OF AMERICA

THE THREAD THAT BINDS US

LAURA & AIDEN

GILLIAN & TERRY

STELLA & STAN

In loving memory of my dear brother-in-law
Aiden McDonald 2/10/2019

ACKNOWLEDGMENTS
Sisters:

Stella Rothwell Rendowski

Laura Rothwell McDonald

Kailey Brewer............. History of the Farington Lodge.

Aileen Daum...............Whose inspiration convinced me to write another book.

Author Roy Sanders.... Who told me I had another story in me.

Mike Sand...................The keeper of the keepsakes, for preserving all the old family photo's

Terry Rose...............For his patience

THIS BOOK WAS WRITTEN FOR MY THREE SONS
MIKE, MARK, AND STEVE.
AND MY SISTERS LAURA AND STELLA.

NORTH WEST ENGLAND

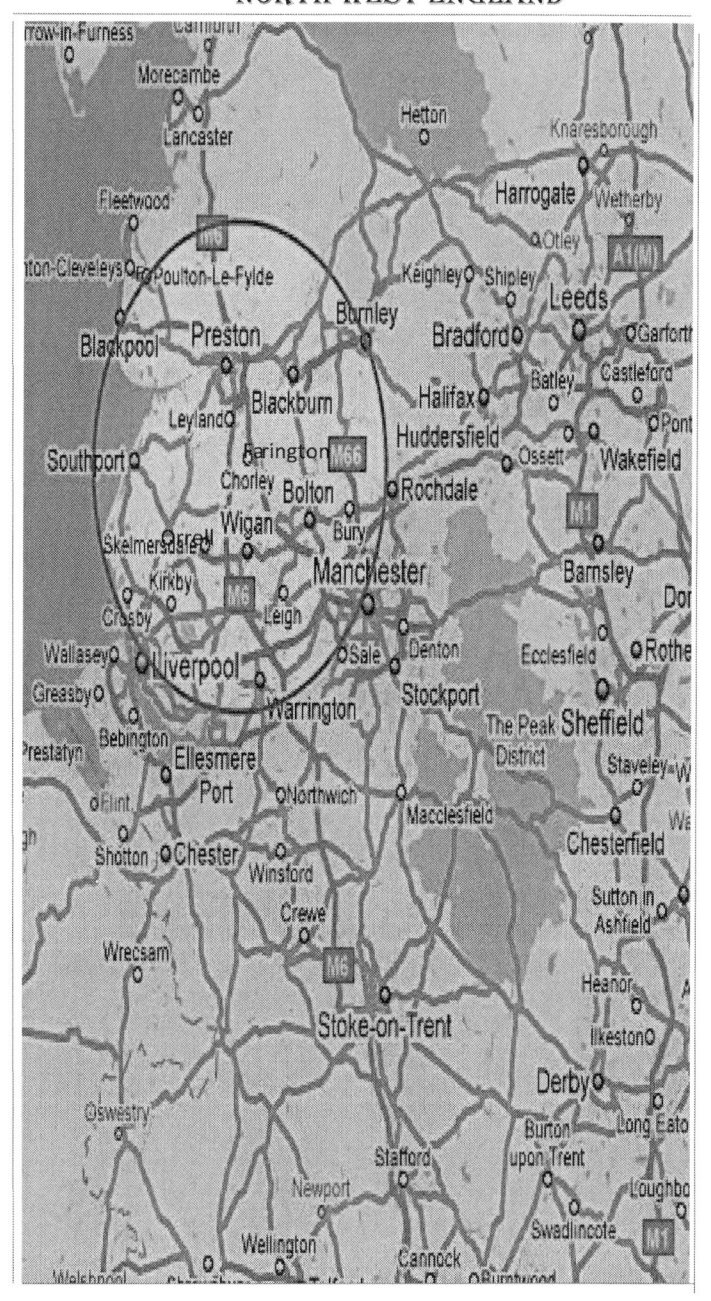

1

GREAT BRITAIN

Great Britain is a tiny island country in the Atlantic Ocean and is separated from the European mainland by the English Channel.

It comprises of the nations of England, Scotland, Wales and Northern Ireland.

There are numerous bare and isolated small islands off the Scottish coast and the well populated Channel Islands, consisting of the Isle of Jersey, Isle of Guernsey, and the Isle of Wight located in the English Channel between England and France.

If you are in Britain you can never be more than eighty-four miles away from the sea, and if the weather was warm and tropical, it would be the holiday, paradise capital of the world.

Unfortunately, Britain's location on the world map puts it close to the Arctic circle, with the upper most tip of Scotland and the southernmost tip of Greenland being just about on the same latitude.

And since there is no land mass which to shelter it from the cold Atlantic, the weather patterns make it a very chilly, wet country.

Consequently, winters are wet and cold and only occasionally does it get cold enough for snow.

July and August can often get into the seventies and sometimes wonderful, cloudless skies can give temperatures even higher than that.

The gulf stream sweeps warm waters past the western coast and brings some warmth to the land and prevents Britain from freezing over in the winter and is the reason for its fairly constant, rainy climate.

Because of this climate, Great Britain is famous for its green pastures, thick forests and blooming shrubs and flowers.

Rhododendrons and Lilac bushes can grow to great heights, and in spring and summer the countryside is alive with color. And the famous English Rose grows prolific in almost everyone's garden.

Even though the country is only eight hundred and thirty-eight miles in length, the temperature difference from the northern tip of Scotland to the southern tip of England's Lands' End in Cornwall can be a difference of thirty degrees on the same day.

But no matter where you are, there is always a chance of rain, and suddenly you can go from a glorious sunny day to biting winds with clouds blustering across the sky, dropping copious amounts of rain on you, so no matter where you are, there is always a chance of rain, and an umbrella is a necessary part of our wardrobe.

2

SISTERS

Even though my sisters and I live hundreds of miles apart, there is a thread that binds us together; that thread is a memory.

Growing up, my sisters and I were very close. They were someone to whisper secrets to, share laughter or shed a tear with. Someone with whom I could share my happiness or times of sorrow. Someone I could always count on.

Don't get me wrong; it wasn't all buttercups and daisies. We had our disagreement's, and that's putting it mildly. Even a few knock-down, drag-out fights. But on the whole, I'd say we got along very well.

And even though there was a fair amount of sibling rivalry, there was also a fierce loyalty, and everyone knew that if you took on one of us, you took on all three.

I have lots of memories, albeit a little sketchy, of when we three sisters were growing up in post-war England.

Those memories we shared are the thread that binds us together today.

Some memories are frighteningly real, some, maybe someone else's memory that got stuck in my mind as my own, some even a little wishful thinking and well, some just outright exaggeration.

But as I was trying to recall a few of them, it was amazing how my train of thought brought more and more to the surface.

With the help of my sisters, Laura and Stella, we came up with this:

Collective, collaboration of the shared *'Do You Remember When's....'* of three sisters growing up in post-war England.

As we shared the memories of our young lives in that post war era, I realized how differently each one of us looked at things back then.

Some memories were shared by all three, some only by each individually.

Some, with just a jog from each other, made a memory, that had been lying dormant for years, amazingly clear.

But we all agreed how amazing the innocence and resilience of us as children gave us the ability to make it through the most trying of times.

3

FIRST MEMORIES

England in the years following the war was very different, in many ways, from the England of today. The most obvious difference was in the physical landscape of the country and in the character of its people.

When I was young, the legacy of the war was still evident everywhere you looked, especially in the major cities.

Particularly in war torn London, because it was the primary seat of government and in the cities of Manchester and Liverpool, because they were the hubs of industry and Liverpool a vital port.

There were many vacant bomb-sites and unrepaired houses everywhere and the countryside was peppered with war-time military bases, many just abandoned.

But this was just normal to us, we had never known anything different.

For most of my early years, everyday life was strongly influenced by the war, so I have tried to tell this story through the eyes of my sisters and I growing up in that post-war era, not as adults looking back on the past.

My first memory, well, I had to have been younger than two years old because my Dad was still away in the war.

I have a hazy memory of sitting in my pram, my Mother sitting on our front wall idly pushing me back and forth, my older sister Laura playing nearby.

My Mother was waiting for her sister, my Auntie Lucy, who was coming to say goodbye. She was leaving for America with her son Paul to join her husband, John Maples.

Auntie Lucy made the long trip by bus to visit us, and I can still remember her walking up the street, a headscarf covering her jet-black hair, carrying a large baby, my cousin Paul, on her hip.

She put Paul into my pram while she and my Mother hugged each other, and I vividly remember this huge baby sitting across from me tugging on my toes.

England had stood alone against Hitler for many years while countries in Europe toppled like dominos until she was joined by a very powerful ally, the United States of America.

John Maples was one of those Americans, powerful, invincible, or so he thought.

John was injured while fighting in Europe and sent to Manchester to recuperate before being sent back home to the states.

His war was over.

My Auntie Lucy, who had joined the WAC's at the beginning of the war, was stationed in Manchester and there she had met and fallen in love with John Maples.

But there were many young women who would raise their babies alone as few men claimed their foreign, wartime offspring.

My cousin Paul was born just one month before me, and he, like me, had never met his dad.

After this meeting, I wouldn't see Paul again for sixteen years, when I too went to America. My Mother wouldn't see her sister When the Americans had first arrived in England, no one knew quite what to expect, because the only Americans we had ever seen were at the picture shows. (*movies*)

Most thought that all American men were tall and either wore ten-gallon hats, running about the wild west on horseback shooting Indians, or were gangsters robbing banks and having shoot outs with cops in Chicago. And that the women all wore silky dresses and danced in dance halls and always smoked cigarettes and wore fur coats.

But my Auntie Lucy assured my Mother that John Maples was a wonderful man, strong and brave and terribly handsome and she was madly in love.

The American government frowned on their soldiers marrying and taking girls from allied countries back to the States. But Auntie Lucy had gotten pregnant and after a hasty marriage applied for passage to the U.S.A.

After two years of waiting, permission had finally been granted for her and their son Paul to join him in America.

I imagine she had quite a culture shock when she finally got there because John Maples lived in the hills of Tennessee and didn't even have running water, but she didn't know that then.

She made the trip across the ocean on the Queen Mary while it was still rigged as a troop ship.

There were many young English women with babies making that trip across the Atlantic. Those English girls just couldn't resist the American

GI's.

for longer than that.

My second memory: I was two years old when I finally met my Dad.

My Mother was pregnant with me when he had been called up to serve in the army. He didn't come back home for over two years.

My Mother always referred to him as George so, in my early years, I didn't know he was also called Dad.

We found out he was our Dad from our Grandma Rothwell, after he came home from the war.

She would say things like, "Where's y'r

Dad?" Or a neighbor would say, "Is y'r Dad 'ome?"

But by that time, I was already in the habit of calling him George, so that was what I did.

He didn't seem to mind though when I called him Dad, in fact, I think he liked it, so I called him that once in a while.

I was a little shy around him at first, but I soon got used to him.

Our Mother, when speaking of him to us, never referred to him as anything but George. She never said, *'your Dad'*, so we would, my two sisters and I, more often than not, refer to him as George for the rest of his life.

4

MISS-FORTUNE OF WAR

On September 3rd, 1939 England finally declared war on Germany. She was now in a fight for her life.

Much of Europe was already in the hands of the Nazi's. The conquest of Britain was their final goal.

My Dad was thirty years old and married.

He was a foreman at the Leyland Rubber Works where they produced tires for motor cars and had been there for several years. The plant was very important to the war effort, producing tires for war time vehicles

My Dad's job was secure. The chances of him being called up were slim.

In 1941 my Mother became pregnant with her first child. My sister Laura was born in May 1942. The war was in full swing.

Many young men volunteered to fight;

others waited to be called up in the Armed Forces.

At first, they were single, eighteen to twenty-two-year old's, but soon, as the fighting progressed and intensified, and more and more young men lost their lives the need became greater, and older and younger men soon found themselves called upon to fight.

When a very young man volunteered, they seldom asked his age, the need was so great. They took in anyone who was willing to fight whether it was obvious or not they were underage.

Now, misfortune doesn't care much on whom she selects as her next victim, and she spotted George Rothwell from across the factory floor in the form of the plant manager.

"Rothwell, come into my office please."

"Look George, it's mi son, he's turning seventeen, there's a good chance he'll get called up if he doesn't have a job, well you know how it is, it's 'is mum, you know, well 'e's so young. Look I'm real sorry, but I'm going to have to let you go." My Dad wasn't out of work for long.

As un-fair as this was, he had no recourse, and a few weeks later he got the notice in the mail to report for duty.

He read the letter with my Mother sitting across from him at the kitchen table.

He handed it to her and her hands began to shake as she made her way through it.

This was a real and clear sign of Britain's desperation, taking a thirty-year-old married man with a child.

They both kept a brave face for each other.

On the day he was to leave, the neighbors came over to shake his hand and wish him good luck before he left for the train station.

My Mother walked with him, pushing Laura in a pram.

When the train arrived to take him away, they just stood there on the platform. Then they embraced each other, she burying her head into his chest to hide her tears, then he was gone.

My Mother watched the train pull away and she waved as it grew smaller and smaller until it disappeared from view.

Then the long walk home.

Ten years younger than my Dad, barely out of her teens with a young child, she now had to face the war alone.

My Dad, leaving, not knowing what his future held. Would he survive? Would she? Would they ever see each other again?

My Mother decided she would wait for a better time to tell him she was pregnant again.

This is my Mother's memory.

He was eventually sent to India and slated for the invasion of Burma, which was firmly in the hands of the Japanese.

But, enter the Americans. With the bombing of Pearl Harbor, America was now fully committed to the war.

This probably saved my Dad's life. The invasion of Burma by the British Army was called off at the last minute, as the Americans took over the fighting in the pacific. Very few had been expected to come out of Burma alive.

During those first months, while my Dad was away, my Mother did what she could to survive.

She had always kept to herself, never socializing with her neighbor's, but now she offered help to others in need, even though she herself was having a difficult time coping.

She took in a Czechoslovakian refugee with a young son. They stayed with us for several weeks.

During Nazi Germany's occupation of Czechoslovakia, thousands of citizens fled their homeland, many escaping to England.

Families all across England took in these refugees while they waited for placement in 'Resettlement Camps'.

She spoke no English. She was always afraid. Afraid of noise, afraid of people. A knock at the door would send her into a panic.

She had escaped from a country firmly in the hands of the Nazi's. Death was everywhere.

Her husband had died fighting for freedom.

How had she made her escape? The language barrier was a wall. We never found out.

When it was time for her to leave, she wept and begged to stay, hanging on to my Mother's arm.

Fear of the unknown, alone but for her young son, not knowing who to trust, she had no idea what the future held or what to expect at the camp.

It was impossible to keep track of her, there were so many.

Then another Mother came to stay with her three children, displaced by the bombing raids in London.

But this one was angry all the time, her children unruly. She let it be known every day how she hated northern England and looked upon my Mother as being lower class. My Mother found her very ungrateful so sent her on her way.

Later, after the war, my Mother would often take us with her when she visited an old Polish woman who was living in a small, dingy one room flat near us; she was also a refugee. Her name was Mrs. Deleon.

She had come to England after the liberation of the concentration camp where she had been held for several years.

She was the only survivor in her whole family. Her parents, husband and children, her brothers and sister and their families, were all gone at the hands of the Nazi's.

When she had first entered the camp, the families were separated and she would not know until liberation day that none but her had survived.

Her walls were covered with the photos, brown with age, of her lost family, snap-shots taken years ago, hidden and cherished through her years in the camp and now hanging there to remind her of her losses.

She had survived but was just waiting to die. Why so many had died and she had lived haunted her.

All the while my Mother was living in her own private hell.

Farington, the town in which we lived, though a rural area, was in the direct flight path across the English Channel to Liverpool, an extremely vital port, which put us at risk.

Many supply ships and troop carriers were sunk in Liverpool harbor, by not only the German bombers but also by the German U-Boats that patrolled the deep waters like circling sharks, ready to pounce as ships came in and out of the harbor.

American soldiers also came into Britain through Liverpool.

Decoy fires were lit along the coast, trying to attract the German bombers to open country, like a moth to the flame. Trying to save this crucial port.

But in spite of this, Liverpool suffered astounding losses. Liverpool was second only to London in the loss of human lives.

A heavy, four-engine bomber was used by the Germans allowing for destructive, strategic bombing and whole city blocks were destroyed by a single bomb.

Much of the technology we use today was just in the early stages in the 1940's, and without GPS or radar they flew over England by sight alone and many German pilots got lost along the way and so dropped their bombs on many insignificant areas. So, no matter where you lived, a stray bomb was always a possibility.

As well as air raid shelters, train stations, which were underground, were often used to escape the nightly bombings.

At the wailing of the sirens, my Mother would rush off to a place of safety, the streets a tangle of people all running in the same direction. Some carrying babies, others precious possessions, maybe a photo album, maybe their life savings.

Some with nothing but themselves.

Once in the shelter, bodies packed tightly together. Stillness. They watched each other and waited for their demise, or the all-clear, all looking like monsters in their gas masks and for the very young, a baby gas bag.

I cannot imagine her fear. The burden of having the responsibility of two babies.

After the all-clear, should she stay or should she leave? If she left would she still have a place to go home to. But, after hearing of an air raid shelter that had taken a direct hit, with all occupants perishing, she decided to take her chances at home, never stepping foot in an air-raid shelter again.

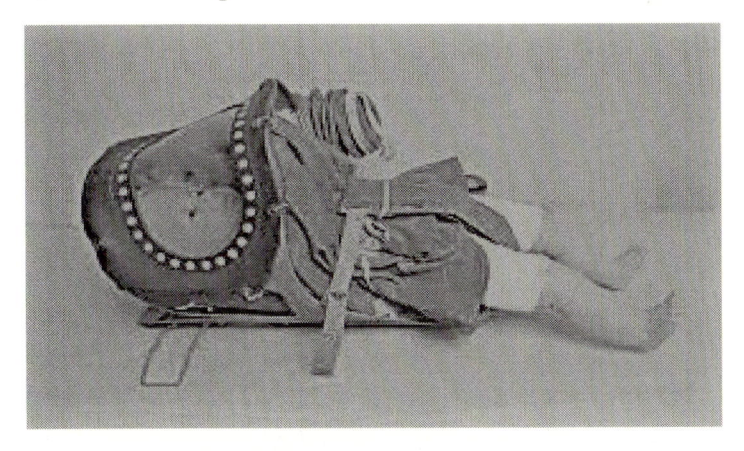

A baby gas bag

Those gas masks and that baby gas bag hung in our pantry for many years after the war, like some gruesome keepsake.

Now when the sirens started to blare, she just sat on the bed and waited, her two babies shoved hurriedly underneath, waiting for an errant bomb to be dropped inadvertently, wailing and whistling on its way to earth that would make the little village of Farington an accidental target.

Until the sirens, signaling the all clear and then she, praying for the people in its path and giving thanks that it had missed us.

After the sirens ceased wailing, she would go outside and see the night sky red and orange from Liverpool burning.

Large spot lights crisscrossed the night sky over every major city, to help make the German bombers visible so anti-aircraft guns on the ground could try and intervene before they could reach their target.

But there was always a possibility that if the bomber flew through the spotlight and took a direct hit, exploding in the sky, that there was a danger of falling debris raining down, and fires were commonplace.

Barrage balloons, a large unmanned blimp, was used to defend against aircraft attacks by raising them aloft on cables, like huge kites, to pose a collision risk, making the bombers approach riskier. These also became a familiar sight over Liverpool and we would often see them

Transporting Barrage Balloons   *Barrage Balloons over Liverpool*

18

drifting by, being pulled by lorries, heading that way.

'Blackout' was strictly adhered to.

Every house had thick, heavy blackout curtains or their windows were painted black. No street lights burned, no vehicles had their lights on. Total darkness.

The, *'no lights what-so-ever'* policy was strictly adhered to as any visible light seen from the air could become a target.

However, despite the *'blackout'* being strictly enforced, and the decoy fires along the coast burning nightly, German planes were still able to decimate Liverpool.

I myself have no recollection of these events. These were also my Mother's memories, memories she could never seem to get rid of.

Memories that would haunt and define her for the rest of her life.

5

HOME FROM THE WAR

The endless months of stress and worry finally took their toll on my Mother and even though she fought on bravely, her mind did everything possible to escape reality, or at least postpone it, and she sunk lower and lower into a depilating depression, becoming so ill she could no longer take care of Laura and I.

Since she was not prone to socializing with her neighbor's and with my Dad's family living forty minutes away in Wigan and no phones in those days, communication was virtually impossible, unless you were willing to make the long trip by bus or train, which was risky at best. This left my Mother isolated and alone with two young children, ill-equipped to deal with the horrors of war.

In those dark, black days they didn't recognize stress disorders and her illness was attributed simply to her nerves. But nerves incapacitated her, and she needed help.

When my Mother became ill, our Grandma Rothwell came to help take care of us and the Army gave my Dad a *Dependency Discharge*.

When my Dad first came home, I did not know who he was. I was two years old and had never seen him before.

At first, I didn't like George living in our house, but then Laura said he was a really nice man, so I decided to like him too.

Laura said she remembered him from before he went off to the war.

I soon got used to having him around because he was a very nice man. He didn't say much and was always whistling, and my Mother did seem a little better.

Before he came home, she was always crying, and Grandma Rothwell told us it was just her nerves but that she would be okay now because our Dad was home.

I remember asking Grandma Rothwell if he was really our Dad, because our Mother hadn't told us yet and Grandma said, "Don't be daft, a'course he's yur Dad."

And I asked her, "Should I call 'im Dad?"

"Ye', you can call 'im Dad if you want."

So, I started to call him Dad, but once in a while I still called him George. It seemed strange calling him Dad, because my Mother always called him George.

He didn't seem to mind when we called him Dad, but he never said one way or another.

I remember, after he had first returned home, looking out of our back window and seeing him trimming our hedges.

He was attacking the hedge with reckless abandon, green leaves flying everywhere, on his shoulders, in his hair, and he was whistling loud and clear.

He turned and a big smile lit up his face. He looked happy.

I asked my Grandma Rothwell, "What's that man George doing cutting our 'edge?"

She replied, " 'cause it's 'i's 'ome; they're 'is 'edges."

6

THE HOME GUARD

When my Dad first came home from the war, he joined the Home Guard.

He was a volunteer and helped guard England in case the Germans came.

Most people thought that an invasion was inevitable, and the Home Guard was considered the last line of defense.

His duties were to man roadblocks, guard factories and explosive stores, and to fight the Germans with everything possible when they arrived.

My Mother and most of the population, thought it could happen any day and everyone lived in fear.

They didn't say *'if'* the Germans came but rather *'when'* they came. We were always scared in those days, and I clung to my sister Laura for comfort.

In the pantry where we kept our food, was where the gas masks and the baby gas bag were hanging on a nail, right next to the gas meter.

Laura told me that when my Mother heard the sirens, she would put me in the bag, put one mask on herself and then one on her.

Laura said it was just in case an airplane dropped a bomb on us, so we wouldn't die, and we had to wear the masks, and I had to be in the bag on account of the Germans put gas in their bombs.

I don't remember ever being put in that bag let alone have a bomb drop on us.

To Hitler, England was the ultimate prize. Most of Europe was by now under his command and all that remained was the tiny island country of Great Britain. But he did not count on the stoic British people.

He could not invade us by sea; we were to well-defended on land. His only option was by air.

He conducted a strategic bombing campaign, primarily against London in the south and other major cities in the north, targeting populated areas, factories and dock yards.

Churchill retaliated by bombing Berlin and this proved to be the turning point in the war.

The Germans were utterly stunned by the British air-attack on Hitler's capital city. They had thought themselves invincible. It was the first time bombs had ever fallen on Berlin.

Hitler was outraged and in retaliation bombed Briton for a total of fifty-seven consecutive nights.

People would spend the nights in their basements, underground railway stations or in air raid shelters, some never bothering to go back home for days on end.

Hitler's intention was to break the morale of the British people so that he could pressure

Churchill into negotiating for peace on his terms.

However, the bombings had the opposite effect, bringing the British people together to face a common enemy.

Encouraged by Churchill's frequent public appearances and radio speeches, the people of Britain became determined to hold out indefinitely against the Nazi onslaught.

'Business as usual,' could be seen everywhere, written in white chalk on boarded-up shop windows.

The German air raids killed thousands of British civilians, and left even more homeless.

The little village of Farington, where we lived, was in a fairly rural area so we didn't see much of the damage inflicted on other parts of the country, but we were later told that there had been an underground tank factory not far from us. If true this was a very well-kept secret indeed, because, not only did the Germans not find out about it but neither did the local citizens.

Whenever my Mother heard an airplane flying overhead, she would start running around screaming, even when my Dad said it was one of ours, but she wouldn't listen and rushed to put us under the bed again just in case, and we would all be crying and screaming too with my Dad trying to calm everyone down.

Our house was never bombed but my Dad said that a bomb had dropped near one of his mate's house and it had been knocked down by the blast and the whole family had to go live with his Mum.

The Home Guard was made up of men who were either too young or too old to be in the war or, men like my Dad who had come home on a *Dependency Discharge.*

He didn't get paid for being in the Home Guard but he said at least he had a chance to do his part to support the war effort.

He was supposed to get a gun and a proper uniform but, like most other men, he only got an armband that said *'L.D.V.'* which stood for Local Defense Volunteer.

Since nobody ever came and told the *L.D.V.'s* what they were supposed to do, my Dad and the rest of the men in our streets, who were also in the Home Guard, started their own unit and going out on patrol.

Because of the strict *'no lights'* policy, on a cloudy night it was black as pitch outside, and if someone had just the slightest gap in their curtains it could be seen for miles and they risked becoming a target.

As a member of the Home Guard it was part of my Dad's duty to go out after dark and check every house in the area to make sure that no light could be seen through any blackout curtains.

He warned us before he went out not to open or peek from behind the curtains because the bombers were looking for any light they could find to drop their bombs on.

One day a bomb was found in a farmer's field nearby but had not blown up. My Dad had called it an *'Unexploded Bomb'* and he had to go help seal off the area so people wouldn't get too close and risk getting blown up if it went off.

He had to wait there all day and all night until somebody came to dismantle it and take it away in a lorry.

My Grandma Rothwell said it was very dangerous as some men who were guarding these bombs would get blown to pieces, and we had been very worried because we had no way of getting in touch with my Dad, so we had no way of knowing what was really happening.

In fact, a large percentage of the fatalities on British soil was caused by these unexploded bombs accidently going off; some were duds, but some were still active, just waiting for a jolt to set them off.

Bombs would be found in farmers' fields, and in construction sites and depth charges would come drifting on to our beaches for many years to come.

And as kids we were always warned, if we found one not to go near it but tell a grown up right away.

When grownups got worried, then we would get worried too, and I would get a stomach ache. It was a big relief when my Dad finally came home from that *'Unexploded Bomb'*.

Although he never got a gun, he was allowed to carry a flashlight, which also worried me because he had told us that the bombers were looking for a light to drop their bombs on and a flashlight was a light. But he assured us that he could hear the bombers before they got there and had plenty of time to turn it off. So that was not so bad, although I would still get a stomach ache until he came back home.

Because of the shortages, we would often run out of coal for our fireplace and it would get quite cold at night, as this was our only source of heating the house.

Since most of the men were off fighting the war, there weren't many men left to deliver it and when they did it was not much, so we only lit a fire when it was really cold.

The man that was delivering our coal was old and had a hard time picking up the bags, but there was nobody left to do it.

He told my Mother when she complained that there wasn't enough to last until the next delivery, that most of the coal was being used to fuel the factories for the war effort and to be grateful for what she got.

When we did run out of coal, some of the men and women in our streets would go out after dark into the Farington Lodge Woods and cut down trees. If caught they risked getting in a lot of trouble as Farington Lodge was private property.

One night while collecting firewood they found the old man that lived in the Lodge laying upside down over his wall, he was so drunk he couldn't stand up. They just turned him right way up, sat him on the ground and carried on collecting wood.

Then they would divide it up, each taking some home for their home fire. Luckily, they never got caught and the man was evidently too drunk to remember and never reported them.

Later that night they all sat around the fire they had built with the wood and had a good laugh.

But my Mother didn't think it was funny because she worried that they would get caught, and we were worried that they might send my Dad back to the war and I had stomach ache all night.

Sometimes a few of my Dad's mates would come over to our house and one of them would bring a bottle of Scotch Whiskey that he had bought on the Black-market and they would all sit around drinking and laughing. My Dad gave us a taste but it was awful.

After we went to bed, we could still hear them and they kept us awake all night with their singing and laughing.

But that was okay, you didn't hear to many people singing and laughing in those days.

7

PEACE IN OUR TIME

Winston Churchill promised the people of Britain, "Peace in our time."

On the 8th of May 1945, the Allies accepted Germany's surrender, the war was over.

This was a week after Adolf Hitler committed suicide.

Cut off the head and the snake will die.

It was called VE Day, *'Victory in Europe'* and everybody went mad, singing and dancing in the streets, celebrating.

They put trestle tables up and down the streets and everybody brought food and they had a party.

My Mother danced around and around and everybody was laughing and cheering.

All over England people were celebrating.

We could turn our lights on at night and leave the curtains open if we wanted too.

Cars could drive with their headlights on and street lights, that had not been damaged, lit up the night sky.

England was alive. We had survived.

THE STREETS CELEBRATING V.E. DAY

But even though it was a happy day, England was far from out of the woods.

For many years to come, our daily lives would be dictated by the events of the war.

There were food shortages everywhere. Clothing shortages, shortages of gas for cooking and shortages of coal for heating our homes.

Everything was rationed, food, clothing, virtually every household item was either in short supply or simply could not be had.

But this could not dampen the spirits of the British people. It beat the alternative and just being released from fear of invasion was enough to sustain us.

Once a month the Postman, (*during the war the Postwoman and then after the war a Postman again*), would deliver our Ration Book. It had a lot of stamps in it. Some were for sugar, some for flour, some for tea, you name it, there was a stamp for it in that ration book.

When your stamps were all used up, you had to wait until the next month when the new Ration Book came out.

There was even a page of stamps for toffee's and chocolate bars, but my Mother told us there was no money for that.

But, once in a while when we were sitting around the fire before bedtime, my Dad would bring out a chocolate bar and share it with us.

That was a very special treat.

Each morning we would check the ration book to see if a toffee and chocolate stamp was missing and if it was, then we knew my Dad had bought one and we would be on our best behavior just in case. We didn't want to take a chance on not getting a piece of chocolate because we had been naughty.

On the days we found a stamp missing we would just sit in front of the fire after our tea and wait, and sure enough off he would go, out of the room and come back with one in his hand and we all sat around the fire savoring a piece of that dark, creamy chocolate bar.

My Dad, even though he didn't say much, was the silent force in those early days of our upbringing.

He taught us how to put on our clothes the right way and what shoe went on what foot and how to tie our shoe laces. He even taught me how to knit and, best of all, he taught me how to whistle.

If one of us would wake in the middle of the night with a tummy ache or because of a bad dream it was always our Dad that would come in and check on us. He showed us that there were no Germans hiding under the bed and he would leave a light on in the hallway.

We knew a lot of what had gone on during the war, not because grownups explained things to us, but rather that's all they ever talked about, so we heard everything and drew our own conclusions.

Consequently, our understanding of what had really happened was very confused.

I was never sure who these Germans were or why they had wanted to bomb our house.

When we did ask a question, it was usually answered by, *"Little children should be seen and not heard."*

In retrospect I wonder how many of my memories were my own experiences or events that I had overheard.

As war babies we did not have any recollections of life before the war or understanding of the true trauma we were living in or the impact the war had on everyone's life.

The hardships that were experienced by adults were to us quite normal.

8

AND THEN THERE WERE THREE

When I turned three and Laura was five, our Mother told us she was going to have another baby. A brother, she said, and they were going to name him William. This, incidentally was the same name she had picked out for Laura and I before she found out we were girls.

When we asked her when the baby was coming, she said in a few months. I wondered why they couldn't pick him up any sooner, but she said he was not ready yet.

When I saw my Mother's tummy getting big, she said that was the new baby growing in her stomach. I was amazed and wondered how it was going to get out.

Today everything would have been explained and the pregnancy shared with the baby's siblings, but not so with us, it was all a great mystery.

When we heard our Dad telling our Mother that she might have another girl, I wonder why, because I thought they had already ordered a boy.

They brought the cot down from the attic, the one that I used to sleep in and put it in their bedroom to get ready for William.

We were all getting really excited but I still couldn't understand how they were going to get him out of my Mothers tummy.

About a couple of months before the baby was to be born the midwife started coming to our house once a week to examine my Mother.

But then the midwife informed my parents that she was going away on holiday and asked if she could bring the baby early. It was only three weeks, no harm would come to the baby, she told them.

They didn't really want to but my Mother was afraid to have the baby without a midwife present so they agreed.

When the midwife arrived at the house, the day the baby was to be born, my Dad told us to go outside and play.

We were really excited and could hardly wait to see our new brother.

After what seemed like hours my Dad finally came to get us so we could see the new baby. Then he told us the new baby was a girl and she was going to be called Stella. It was not the longed-for son after all.

I think Laura and I were a little disappointed that it was not the promised brother, but my Dad seemed to be happy so we were too. Stella was very small when she was born and got pneumonia right away and there was much worry and concern.

My Grandma Rothwell said it was because she had come too early and her lungs where not properly formed.

They kept her in their bedroom all bundled up in her little blue blanket that had been bought especially for William, and we were not allowed to go see her.

Grandma Rothwell came to help out again.

It took a while but finally Stella started to get better and we were at last able to play with her.

Grandma Rothwell went back home again.

Stella was a happy baby from the start and would smile at us when we would peek over the side of the cot. We would play peek-a-boo and she would laugh out loud and try and see where we would jump up next.

Our Mother said she was a good baby because she didn't cry very often. She told me, when I was a baby, I cried all the time and she didn't get a moments rest.

Stella slept in the cot next to their bed for the first few months but after a while they brought her cot into our bedroom and she started sleeping in our room.

She was a good baby and would make funny gurgling noises and play with her toes before she went to sleep. She never kept us awake at night.

My sisters and I were very different from each other, not only in appearance but also in personalities and temperament. Which is still very evident to this day.

Laura with her black curly hair and dark brown eyes often turned heads and other mothers would bend down and pinch her cheeks remarking on how pretty she was and what beautiful hair she had. But Laura could turn that pretty face into a scowl in an instant if she did not get her way, and would more than likely talk back. My Mother said she was *'Argumentative'*. She also told her she was her favorite and the most beautiful of us three girls.

I was pretty generic, I had plain brown hair, that was braided most of the time. It was neither straight enough to gleam in the sunlight nor curly enough to render me adorable. My features were certainly pleasant but not enough to be remarked upon as beautiful, but I do have hazel eyes bordering on green and my Mother said they were my best feature. My Mother said I never really cared what people said and if I was shouted at, I would just let it go in one ear and out the other. She said I was a *'Cold Fish'* and that things would just roll off me *'like water off a duck's back'*. She also told me I was her favorite and the most beautiful of us three girls.

Now Stella, she was a very beautiful baby, she had a peachy complexion, blonde hair that did gleam in the sunlight and baby blue eyes and she would melt hearts with her smile and chubby cheeks, but she was also very sensitive and at the slightest rebuke she would scrunch up her face and cry, which, I must admit was not very often. My Mother said she was such a good baby, *'Sweet as Sugar'*, and *'Could do no Wrong.'* And she told her she was her favorite and was the most beautiful of us three girls.

You see where I am going with this?

After a while we cottoned on to the fact that she told each one of us that we were her favorite and the most beautiful and it was usually after one of us had been exceptionally good, which I must confess, as far as Laura and I were concerned didn't happen very often.

So, we decided for a laugh that the one who was the favorite at any given time be given the *'Number One Spot'*. And the one who had been the naughtiest was relegated to *'Number Three'*.

Stella was usually number one and Laura mostly number three and I usually hovered around the number two position, once in a while dropping to number three.

When we got older and lived continents away from each other, my Mother sort of took this to the extreme and when we sisters talked to each other on the phone we would try and ascertain in what position we were currently in and have a good laugh.

No offence Mom.

Through the years, as I realized all my Mother had been through, I vowed to forgive her for any injustice she heaped upon me. Whether real or imagined.

9

GLOUSTER AVE

Farington, a sleepy little village in Lancashire County in northern England was a great place to grow up, and although only sixteen miles south of industrial Wigan the landscape was not scarred nor the air polluted by cottons mills and coal mines.

Our house sat in a street with three other streets surrounded by a farmer's fields. Two streets were back to back houses with the one street across the top.

The back to back houses were separated, by what is commonly known as an alley, but we always just called it *'The Backs'*. The street across the top, which we referred to as the *'Tops'* was bordered by the farmers' fields, except for a little oasis of open field directly behind our house which was referred to as the *'Back Field'*, and, an open area just to the right of the top street which we, not surprisingly called the *'Top Field'*.

In the top field the farmer had made his fence out of old doors.

Laura always said that if we went through one of those doors we would be in Fairyland and that the fairies would keep us forever and we would never be able to come back home again. I didn't believe it for one minute, but I kept my distance just in case.

Our house and all the houses in the streets were semi-detached with a little wall separating the front gardens and a privet hedge separating the back gardens.

My Dad loved to garden and after he got home from the war, our front garden became a profusion of Lupins in every color imaginable. And in the front corner a Laburnum tree that in the spring would be dripping with tiny yellow flowers.

It was great having a Dad.

All the houses in our little community were built of red brick and the only difference was the color of the doors and window frames.

At the bottom of the Streets was the main road which was called Stanfield Lane and if you went to the left you could go to Leyland and to the right into Preston.

On the other side of the lane was a park with swings, slides and a round-about. Mums would take their children there to play.

Beyond the park was a large open field and once in a while the Cricket Club would have a cricket match there.

At the bottom of the field, separated by a fence, was an old abandoned factory with a dirty reservoir.

To the right of the open field, sitting on a hill was a very large house.

It was called the Farington Lodge. It was quite an imposing place. It was built of red brick that was concealed under a thick blanket of dark green ivy.

Farington Lodge

It had its own apple orchard, grand gardens and woods and somebody very rich lived there.

The whole house and grounds were surrounded by a high, intimidating wall.

But I must admit, after seeing it later in life I realized that it was not that high of a wall, but I guess when you are only a couple of feet tall then yes, it was a high wall, everything being relative.

A long curvy driveway went from the house, through the woods, down to the lane, but you couldn't see it for the trees. We knew about the driveway because we used to play in those woods.

It was strictly forbidden to go in the woods and they had signs everywhere that said we would be prosecuted. We weren't sure what that meant, but we were really careful that nobody saw us go in.

The high wall was hard to climb but the gate was very often left open.

The rich man that lived in the Lodge left the big, double iron gates open when he was in residence, so he wouldn't have to get out of his car to open and close it when he went somewhere in his big motor car.

Once in a while we would see him leave and a man wearing a cap would always be driving.

We were not sure who he was but later I learned he owned Leyland Motors. That was probably where he got his big motor car from.

10

PRESTON MARKET

At the end of the war approximately five million service members in the British Armed Forces were de-mobilized and re-assimilated back into civilian life. This was one of the greatest challenges facing the post-war British Government.

Most men and women were to be released according to their age and number of years served.

Also, a small number of so-called *'key men'* whose occupational skills were vital to the postwar reconstruction were to be released ahead of their turn.

Married women and men aged fifty or more were also given immediate priority.

The release process began on June 18, 1945, about six weeks after V-E Day.

During the next eighteen months approximately 4.3 million men and women returned to civilian life.

The romantic image you have come to know of the handsome returning soldier running into the open arms of his beautiful wife in her little apron and two or three children at her heels couldn't have been further from actual reality.

Most couples had not seen each other in years and the welcoming wife, after years of stress, was usually an aged, frayed woman whom he did not recognize from the woman he had kept alive in his dreams. And that handsome young soldier in uniform was now a weathered and war-torn man.

P.T.S.D, or post-traumatic stress disorder, was known in those days as being shell shocked, and was the biggest obstacle facing returning soldiers in post-war England.

But in this war, not only men suffered but women too. After living under the gun for years, domestic violence, divorce and suicide sky rocketed.

It would be decades before England stabilized herself.

Another consequence of the returning soldiers was a baby boom.

In post-war Britain, the government built numerous new schools and introduced other measures such as free school milk and child benefits to cater to the booming generation.

Many soldiers returning home had difficulty finding work. Positions they held prior to the war were no longer available, having been filled by the next generation that just missed the age of having to serve. And many were just too injured both mentally and physically to work.

Cities all over the country were littered with homeless broken men.

Those that could work took any menial task available to try to eke out a living to put food on the family table.

The Government could not help, there was nothing left. Men had to fend for themselves.

When my Dad came home, he went back to work at the Leyland Rubber Works, but they did not give him his old position back but rather offered him a very menial position as an office person which did not pay enough for us to survive on.

To supplement their income, my Mother and Dad started standing the open Market in Preston on Saturday's selling shoes.

Preston Market in the 1950's

The Market wasn't too bad on a nice day, but nice days are few and far between in England and the sun seldom shines and when it does, offers little warmth, and even though the Market had a covered roof it was open on all sides to the weather and on a cold and rainy day it was downright brutal.

But desperate times call for desperate measures and these were desperate times and everybody did what they could to survive.

They would take us with them once in a while and I hated it. It was so cold and drafty and we had to stay there all day.

So, then my Grandma Rothwell started coming over to our house again to take care of us.

Both my parents had good heads on their shoulders and in spite of the harsh working conditions were quite successful.

Shoes in the stores were usually beyond the reach of the working class and the best place to shop was the Markets.

My Dad offered a fair price and quality shoes and they soon got a good reputation as a place to buy shoes at a fair price.

11

THE LOST GENERATION

With the passage of time the citizens of England slowly felt the burden of war lifting from their shoulders.

Their stoic resilience, though cracked was not broken and although they still were experiencing shortages and rationing, they were slowly returning to a life of normalcy.

Dads, sons and husbands started to come home, but, unfortunately, many would not. England later referred to this era as the *lost generation*.

We were lucky, our Dad came back all in one piece. Many did not return and most that did suffered from great trauma both physically and mentally.

My Grandma Rothwell said that many men came back missing arms and legs. In my young ignorance of what had really happened, I often wondered what the Germans did with all those arms and legs that were left behind?

My friend Eileen waited day after day for her dad to come home.

"He's in the hospital getting better," she told us, "but he'll be home soon."

Days stretched into months, "soon," she would answer when we inquired.

But suddenly the waiting was over. "He's coming home," she screamed running down the street towards us.

They brought him home in a Red Cross ambulance. Everybody on the Streets was there to greet him and they cheered and sang, "For he's a jolly good fellow." He was a war hero.

They had put him back together in the hospital but he seemed all jumbled up, like they left pieces off or couldn't remember where each piece was supposed to go.

His face was wrinkled like burned paper and he only had holes with his eye balls poking out. And they forgot to put his lips and ears back on.

He wore a cap, but I knew he had no hair underneath. His jacket was buttoned all the way to the top and hung on his shoulders like they had given him the wrong jacket, two sizes too big. I could see his hands hanging from the sleeves and one hand had no fingers.

He held a walking stick with the other hand and waved at the crowd with his fingerless one.

He had a big shiny, silver medal pinned to his jacket

Eileen, who had been at the front of the crowd looked back at her mum when she saw the man emerge from the ambulance and started shrinking back into the crowd.

But her mum held on to her and would not let her break free.

"No," she screamed, "that's not my dad, where's my dad?"

She glanced at the open door of the ambulance as though still expecting him to emerge. Then she started crying and wrestled herself free of her mother's grasp and ran away.

Her mother said, to no one in particular, "Just leave 'er be, sooner or later she'll get used to 'im." We wanted to leave too but our Mother and Dad made us stay because he was a real war hero.

Eileen's dad was a pilot and my Dad told us he had been shot down over the sea and the only reason he didn't die was because the salt water stopped his burns from getting infected.

Death, pain and destruction had touched everyone's life in one way or another and adults did not try and shield their young from the realities of the war or its consequences.

I had nightmares about Eileen's dad for a long time after that.

Finally, Eileen did get used to him, soon he was just another dad in the Streets.

Once, when I was over at Eileen's house, her dad said something to me and his mouth didn't move on account of the burns, but I still understood what he said.

I tried not to stare and didn't know where to look but then he said, "It's alright."

When any grownups got together, they always talked about the war, even long after it was over. I guess they didn't have anything else to talk about and every conversation began with, *during the war*, and if we were sitting around and could hear them, we would groan, "Oh no, not another war story."

Which reminds me of a funny incident years later. I was sitting at the dinner table with my three teenage sons and started to tell them of something that had happened to me during the war, and one of them groaned, "Oh no Mom, please, not anther war story."

Some things never change.

12

SHOES

With the shoe selling business going well and more money to spend, life got a little easier for the Rothwell's, although our Mother would still get fits of crying and very often didn't feel well and take to her bed.

My Dad was still at the Rubber Works, but then, making the boldest decision of his life, announced he was leaving the factory and going to sell shoes six days a week.

He bought a little car, a Bond Mini, to transport the shoes to the Market. We had the first car in the streets, and we would often have shoes stacked from floor to ceiling in our hallway.

My Mother started going with him each day and since both our parents would be gone our Grandma Rothwell came over again to watch us.

A great memory I have of Grandma Rothwell was of her baking pies and the house would have this wonderful aroma all day.

Sometimes blackberry, which we had picked and sometimes rhubarb from our back garden and if they were available an apple pie.

She would let us climb up on chairs while she made the pastry on a board on the kitchen table. We had little tin pans and when she cut out the pie crust, she would sprinkle sugar on the left over pieces and we would press them into the tins to make a crust and then she would put a dollop of jam in the middle and bake them when she baked her pie. We called them jam tarts and they were so good straight out of the oven piping hot.

One time, when we came in Grandma Rothwell was baking a pie. We had dirty hands from playing outside but that didn't stop Laura from reaching in and pulling off a piece of pastry while Grandma was still rolling it. Grandma shouted at her and when Laura jumped back, she accidently tore the pastry.

Grandma was fighting mad and shouted at her again and called her a cheeky monkey.

Then Laura told Grandma to, *"Bugger off."* That's because Laura was *'Argumentative and always talked back."*

Well, Grandma Rothwell picked up that rolling pin and Laura took off in a flash. I was right behind her. I didn't want to be anywhere near that flying rolling pin.

Out of the back door we ran, down the garden and out of the back gate with Grandma Rothwell hot on or heels.

She didn't catch us though, we were too fast for her, on account of her being old, and when we got out of breath we stopped running and thanked our lucky stars that we hadn't been killed. She called after us, shouting, "Just you wait 'til y'r Dad gets 'ome, I'm telling 'im what you said," and she did.

Laura got the strap for being rude to our Grandma.

Now the strap was not really the torturous instrument it sounds like. It was about a foot long and maybe an inch wide and was made of leather. My Dad had it hanging on a nail by the kitchen table.

Mostly he would use it as a threat, like when we were naughty, he would say, "Do you want me to get the strap?"

Now, for really bad infractions, like telling Grandma Rothwell to bugger off, the strap was something that could not be avoided.

The strap usually meant a slap across the palm of your hand, it didn't really hurt all that much, although we pretended it did so my Dad would think that one was punishment enough.

But no matter how much Laura wailed and carried on she still got another for disrespect.

Most times though, when we were naughty, Grandma Rothwell would say she was going to tell our Dad but mostly she never did. She was really a nice Grandma.

But my Grandma, being old, soon found the bus ride from Wigan too much for her, so our Auntie Annie started coming instead.

My Dad was one of six siblings, my Auntie Annie being the oldest. Then there was Uncle John, Uncle Tom and then my Dad. After him was my Uncle Harold and lastly Auntie Edith.

I never met my Grandfather Rothwell because he'd drowned in Liverpool Harbor when my Dad was just a boy.

They were a kind and loving family but, on account of them all living in Wigan, forty minutes away by bus and with no telephone services yet, we didn't see much of them except at Weddings, Funerals, Christenings, Christmas and the occasional visit on Sundays.

My Auntie Annie had just lost her husband, my Uncle David.

Much later I learned that he had a bad fall from his bicycle on the way home from work one day and had suffered some brain damage. He became despondent over his inability to work and earn a living. So, he had gone down to the outhouse, when Auntie Annie was not home, stood on the toilet, tied the chain around his neck and jumped down. My Auntie Annie found him a few hours later but he was already dead.

Since nobody actually told us what happened and how he had died and we had only overheard sketches of the guarded truth, we were left with our own understanding of what had happened.

My interpretation, at that young age was, that Uncle David was standing on the toilet seat, became tangled in the chain and fell to his death.

I often wondered how that chain got accidently wrapped around his neck and just what in the heck was he doing standing on the toilet seat in the first place. After that I was always very careful when I visited the toilet.

Now that her husband was dead Auntie Annie no longer had any income and with my cousin Edith, her daughter, at Grammar School having past her 11+ (I will explain the 11+ later) she found herself in dire financial straits. So, my Mother and Dad asked her if she wanted to watch us while they were at the Market and she gladly accepted.

They paid her a wage and covered her bus fare back and forth from Wigan. So, it worked out well for everybody.

I liked my Auntie Annie watching us. She would make us little butty's (*sandwiches*) and a cup of tea for our lunch and once in a while made us potato pancakes.

She didn't mind if we were gone a long time when we were out playing or if we were late for lunch and she took really good care of Stella, except on a rainy day when we had to play inside, then she would bring Stella over and plop her down on the floor and tell us we had to let her play with us.

It wasn't so bad though; except she would get into everything and would tear down the blanket we had put up to make a den.

Our favorite place to play, on a rainy day was in the panty. The pantry was the little room where the gas meter was with the gas masks and baby gas bag hanging on a nail and where they kept all the food.

The gas meter was a red box with a slot and a dial on the front and big pipes coming up through the floor. When we were out of gas the dial would read empty and it was time to put a shilling in the slot to get more gas, then the dial would go back up to full.

One day when we were playing in there, I found a shilling under the meter. Somebody must have dropped it and it had rolled under there.

I cried out that I had found a shilling but Laura, putting a finger to her lips, shhh'ed me and told me to hand it over and then she put it in her pocket.

After it stopped raining, we told Auntie Annie we were going outside to play.

As soon as we were outside, we high-tailed it down to the Grocery Shop.

When we got there nobody else was inside the shop except for the shopkeeper standing behind her counter; she was always mean and never smiled.

"And what can I do for you two," she said folding her arms across her ample bosom.

Laura pulled the shilling out of her pocket reached up and put it on the counter and said.

"Two chocolate bars please."

"Where's y'r ration stamps," she asked.

"Uh, we don't 'ave any."

"Well wi'out any stamps I can't give yu any chocolate bars, now can I? 'cause it's against the law."

Laura was mad and reached up to retrieve our shilling, but that shopkeeper scooped it up, just like that.

"'Ey that's our shilling," exclaimed Laura, "give it back."

But the shopkeeper just reached down under the counter and pulled out two, one penny lollipops, put them on the counter and said, "'Ere."

"That's not fair," shouted Laura.

56

"Take it or leave it, or I tell y'r mum you had a shilling, 'cause 'eaven only knows where you got it from," she replied.

What could we say? If she told our Mother we knew we would have a lot of explaining to do, so we picked up the lollipops and headed for the door.

But Laura, being *'Argumentative'* and *always talking back*, hollered at her, "Y'r naught but a bloody thief." As for me, I didn't say anything, you know because of that, *water off a duck's back'* thing.

Well, that shopkeeper flew out from behind her counter, but we were too fast for her and were already off and we knew she wouldn't tell our Mother on account of she had stolen our shilling.

13

SCHOOL

I think we all have strong memories of our first day at school, and I am no exception. I was five years old and it was time for me to start.

Now in those days, as it probably is today half of the children can't wait to start school and the other half are scared to death and don't want anything to do with it. I was in the half who couldn't wait to go.

Laura was going into the Third Form and for two whole years I had watched her go off to school wishing I could go too.

Nowadays most children attend pre-school, and all attend kindergarten, so it is not such a shock to their system when they go full time into first grade, but not so with the children the 1950's and 1960s.

There were no pre-schools or nurseries, so for children just turning five years old, their first day at school was a full day.

It was the first time many had been on their own, or away from home.

Consequently, the first day of school was a very traumatic and tearful event for both child and parent!

When Stella started school, four years later, they had *'Infants'*, where you went to school at the age of four for a few hours a day and you got to play with other kids your age, sort of to get you used to being in school.

But they hadn't adopted that when I started so when I went to school for the first time, there I was, just plonked into school full time.

The school year ran from the first Monday in September to mid-July of the following year, the year being broken up into three Terms.

The end of the summer holiday, in September, marked the beginning of the new school year. The first term, which was called the Autumn Term ran until December with two weeks off for the Christmas Holiday. The second Term was from the first week in January until mid-March with two weeks off for Easter, this Term was called the Spring Term. The Summer Term ran from mid-March to mid-July and that was the end of the school year and the beginning of the summer holidays, which were six weeks long.

If you turned five before the beginning of the school year then you started school in September. If you turned five after the beginning of the school year then you had to wait until the following year. So, you could be nearly six before you started school.

Since my birthday was in March, I started school the year I turned five.

School started at eight o'clock sharp and finished at four.

Even though all the kids in my class were about the same age as me, when we changed rooms, or at playtime or lunch time we were just thrown in with all the bigger kids. Which can be quite intimidating for a five-year-old. Especially when you are small in stature like I was. I soon got the nickname half-pint.

But having an older sister in school helped and when I first started, Laura would let me hang out with her and her friends at playtime and lunch time until I got used to it and could hold my own and start to have friends of my own.

My Mother took me to school on my first day. She was pushing Stella in her pram and Laura and I walked along side.

On that first day there was lots of hugging's and crying as expected, because most kids hadn't been separated from their mums before and many had never been away from home.

While some kids clung to their mum's crying, my Mother said, "Well are you okay then?" "Yea, I'm good," I answered.

"Well I'll be off," she said. "make sure you mind your teachers."

And off she went.

Of course, I was okay, but still I was a little put out she didn't stick around a while like the other mothers.

I walked home from school with Laura.

I liked school but found it tiring, because we had to stay there all day.

I started school at Farington Primary in 1949 on Moss Road not far from Leyland.

The first thing they did was give us all the polio vaccine. It was given at school to every child on a cube of sugar.

Measles, German Measles and Mumps were not vaccinated against in those day and most children contracted these diseases in early childhood.

German Measles, or Rubella, can affect unborn babies if contracted during a pregnancy, so if a girl in the class caught German Measles, all the other mums would try and expose their girls to it so they could also catch the disease, to protect them from catching it in their later years.

I never had the measles but Laura did.

Probably the biggest difference from school back then compared to school today was the actual getting there and coming home.

Very few parents had cars in those days to drive their young one's back and forth to school, and there was no such thing as a School Bus, so we were left more or less to our own devices and Laura and I would make the half mile walk back and forth to school along a route no parent would ever allow today.

Most days it was rainy and gray with a chilly wind that blew down the road and bit at your knees and ankles.

When we got to school, we would all report to our home room so the Form teacher could take attendance, and then we would all file into the school hall for assembly.

Assembly would comprise of a Hymn, the singing of our National Anthem and a long talk from the Headmaster about the sins of misbehaving, the importance of learning and what he expected out of us that day.

Since there were no chairs in the hall, we all stood in rows side by side. And since there was no specific place you had to stand you might find yourself standing next to a kid the same height as you or one as big as any adult and I was always watchful in case one of them stepped on me.

Usually though, the big kids would stand in the back, not because they were concerned that the smaller ones couldn't see, but rather so they could be as far away from the Headmaster as possible and able to make a quick retreat when it was over.

It was very often stuffy in that hall and invariably someone would faint. (*English people seem prone to fainting*).

At some point you would hear someone go down and that would often lead to a chain reaction.

When someone fainted, probably because they'd had nothing to eat, the older kids would think it was funny and laugh.

But a quick glass of water and a putting of the head between the knees the unfortunate student would soon be revived and things could continue.

Thank God I was not a fainter.

Our Mother always gave us a bowl of Kellogg's Corn Flakes before we went to school, so we could make it to lunch time, a meal that was provided by the school. Yuck!

We took the basic subjects; Math, English, Geography, Music, History, Biology, Science and P.E, (physical education), which was a split class, one for the boys and one for the girls and since we didn't have any gym clothes, we just removed our outer clothes and did P.E. in our undershirts, knickers or underpants, and bare feet.

To these classes they added dance, which was a mixed class and we had to dance with a boy.

All the girls hated dancing with the boys because they would squeeze or pinch your hand and stand on your toes, sometimes on purpose.

And I always thought boys smelled funny.

My Mother always made sure we had enough to eat and she always dressed us as nice as she could.

Even though she herself had not had much schooling and having spent most of her young life isolated, she was nevertheless an extremely intelligent woman.

Now if we wanted to know what 12 x 12 was or how to spell a word she would say, "Go ask your Dad".

But if you asked her what that word meant you had her full attention. Or, if you wanted to know where Africa or Australia was, she always knew the answer.

Not that we needed to know for school, we had no homework.

But I was fascinated by History and Geography and the Stars and Planets and she knew everything and I could ask her any question about anything and she would spend hours explaining things.

Unfortunately, our teachers didn't seem to interested in these kinds of things. They just wanted you to learn the basics.

But I would spend hours poring over the book of maps and day-dreamed about what different countries were like and how the people lived and about their history.

Books were a wonderful source of knowledge for me, once I learned how to read. I would disappear into a book where I was a happy visitor to all the worlds that sprang full-blown from the printed pages.

I was not so good at math and was never too sure what a noun or pronoun was, so I always seemed a little behind. And the teacher told my Mother I was a daydreamer and needed to pay more attention. I think they thought I was a little slow.

But as I progressed through the coming years, I didn't do too bad and managed to make it through.

I'd always been a neat writer, which the teachers held in high esteem and did well in geography and my favorite, history. But always having your nose in a book didn't seem to give you any merit.

The dress code at school was pretty strict.

Not necessarily the condition your clothes were in, because actually most kids were impoverished and wore the clothes that their siblings had worn. Some on their second hand-me -downs from two siblings above them.

Holes and darned clothes where more the norm, except for those kids whose parents came from the upper class who were always nicely dressed. It was rather how you wore your clothes that counted.

A boy could never wear his shirt outside his pants, and they had to be short pants, coming just above the knees.

The girls had to either wear a dress or a skirt and that had to come just below the knees.

Which, when you think about it, was sort of ridiculous given the cold and wet climate of England and the fact that the majority of us had to walk to school. Everybody arrived with cold knees.

And you must wear socks, no matter how often they had been darned.

We were always dressed nice and my Mother did everything she could to make sure we were well fed and kept warm.

Once a month a ribbon was given out at assembly to the young lady and young gentleman who best represented the youth of England; consequently, the same well-dressed kids got the ribbon month in month out.

Talk about cruel and usual punishment for the less fortunate.

Every month I would work towards that ribbon. I would make sure my shoes were clean and that any darned holes in my socks were not showing.

I convinced my Mother that I needed a cardigan because one of the girls who had won the ribbon twice always wore one.

Day in and day out I wore that cardigan. But I never did get the ribbon.

A couple of other rules were, we had to learn the Nation Anthem by heart. The girls had to learn how to curtsy properly and the boys had to learn how to bow, just in case we came face to face with the King (*King George was still on the throne*). I never did come face to face with him, but if I ever did, you can be sure I knew the correct way to curtsy.

Our writing had to be straight up, it couldn't be sloping one way or the other. And the worst of all, any kids who wrote with their left hand had to learn how to write with their right.

For those left handers that lapsed, a rap on the knuckles with a ruler had the offending student changing hands quickly.

And last but not least, it was deemed by the government that all children were undernourished and due to the deprivations of the war, they were not drinking enough milk, therefore not getting the calcium they needed for strong bones. So, each morning we were given a half-pint bottle of milk.

Yes, we had a half-pint measurement, it was called a Gill, hence my nickname half-pint.

We had to drink the whole thing while the teacher watched to make sure we drank it all, like it or not. In the summer it was always warm and, in the winter, very often frozen.

This was called The School Milk Program, so even if some kids hadn't had any breakfast, which many had not, they at least got their daily ration of milk. So, each morning we were give a half-pint bottle of milk.

Yes, we had a half-pint measurement, it was called a Gill, hence my nickname half-pint.

We didn't drink much milk at home. What milk we did get was on our cereal in the morning and some in a hot cup of tea, which we drank four or five cups of a day.

Most everyone in England drinks tea, even very small children.

What milk we did get was delivered about twice a week, depending on our needs, in glass bottles on our front doorstep. When the bottles were empty, we would put them back outside so the milkman could come and pick them up. We put a note in the empty telling him how many bottles we needed that day.

At first a lady on a horse drawn cart would deliver our milk, but after the war she was replaced by a man. After the war most women went back into the kitchen.

Our milkman always wore a white uniform, which I think may have been different from one dairy to another. He had on a white peaked cap, white overalls and a long white apron.

He would knock on the door on Saturday mornings for payment and put the money into a large leather shoulder bag which had separate pockets for the different denominations of coins so he could make change.

The free school milk program was done away with for kids over the age of seven in 1968 and ended altogether in the year 1971 by Margaret Thatcher who, at the time, was the Secretary of Education.

Every few weeks we were required to visit the school nurse which would break up the daily routine. She would check us for nits *(headlice)*.

All the children in each class would line up to be examined in turn, their hair being combed carefully with a nit comb to see if there was any infestation. If somebody had nits, they were sent home with a note not to come back until the problem was taken care of.

There were also routine eye and hearing tests and visits to the school dentist.

I remember one particular morning. It was an unusually warm day; Laura and I were running to school. We were going to be late.

When they said school started at eight o'clock sharp there was no acceptable excuse for being late. Even for two little girls having had to circumnavigate an angry dog.

We knew we would be in trouble.

When we got there, assembly had already begun, and we expected the worse.

We went through the big front doors as stealthily as possible.

All was quiet in the hallway, the only sound coming from the muted voice of the Headmaster giving his morning speech in the assembly hall.

Walking cautiously down the hallway we were happily surprised to see, possibly due to the warm weather and the stuffiness of the hall, that the doors had been left open. Spying our chance, we sneaked in through the open door. Laura going off to the right where her friends were holding a space for her and I went to the left to try and disappear into the crowd before I was spotted.

Laura gave me a look as if to say, are you alright and I gave her a nod.

I went down about three rows and then pushed my way in through a forest of long legs and knobble knees. Uh oh, I looked up and realized I was in a row with all the big kids, boys!

I kept on moving down the row, then I accidently stood on a foot.

I froze but when I looked up at my victim, I thought I detected understanding in his eyes.

He just sort of hustled me down the row and each boy in turn moved me along. When, I can only assume was about the middle of the row, they made room for me.

The Headmaster must have seen some movement in the back of the room and stopped talking.

Everybody stood stock still, nobody acknowledging the interloper in their midst.

After what seemed like an interminable length of time, he continued on in his drolling voice that nobody was listening to anyway.

I felt myself relax and gave a sigh of relief and a thank you smile to the big boy standing next to me.

As I stood there, surrounded by all those big boys in that hot and stuffy room, I suddenly felt myself sway. It seemed like I was suspended in space for an incredibly long time, although in reality it was probably no more than a split second. The world seemed to slow down around me, and the floor rushed up and I crashed painfully down into oblivion. My last thought was, I'm going to die, right here in this stinking hall.

Then blackness descended.

After some unknowable expanse of time I drifted back into reality, not quite sure what had happened!

It's okay, I'd only fainted. I thought I would just add a little drama to my narrative. So much for being one of those kids that never faints!

Suddenly the darkness no longer swirled around me and when my eyes focused, I was looking up to a dozen pair of eyes staring down at me.

Then a teacher came down the row to see what all the commotion was and bending down pulled me by the arm into a sitting position and said. "What on earth are you doing all the way back here?"

Still sitting on the floor, he made me put my head between my knees and then backed off to be replaced by a lady teacher with a drink of water.

When I was able to stand up, she led me down to the front row were all the short kids where.

The Headmaster glared down at me as if to say, 'how dare a little pip-squeak like you interrupt me.'

After what seem like a long time, everybody settled down, and the Headmaster continued on with his long boring speech.

The older kids could be pretty mean at times but when pitted against a teacher, especially the Headmaster, they would always stand up for you. Of course, that didn't extend into the playground where the general chaos and bullying went on.

But Laura and I could have saved ourselves the trouble. Because we had not been present for attendance in our home room we were written up for tardiness and summarily punished.

Punishment was usually a rap on the knuckles with a ruler or being made to stand in a corner for a while.

14

FARINGTON LODGE

When the school day ended, we rushed home so we could play outside.

In the winter months, night came early, four/five o'clock and we took advantage of what little light we had left. But as winter turned into spring the days grew longer and longer until by mid-summer it stayed light until at least ten o'clock.

We played outside until we heard the familiar high pitch whistle that called us in.

We had a lot of friends in the streets and although I can recall what they looked like I can remember only a few names.

There was Bobby Dearden, Kathleen Oakley, Billy Marsden, Eileen Crowsdale and Tubby Trelfal, just to name a few. I am not sure what Tubby Trelfals real name was because we always just called him Tubby on account of he was fat.

We were a motley crew. Dressed in scraggy playing out clothes, many of us in hand-me-downs and more often than not wearing our black rubber Welly Boots because more often than not it was wet and rainy.

When it was nice, which wasn't very often, we would play on our roller skates.

Four wheels strapped to your shoes. Real ankle busters.

About once a month the Rag-and-Bone man would wander through our streets on his horse and cart.

We would jump on the back and ride around, jumping off when he headed off down the lane. Or we would hang on the back and let him pull us round on our roller skates. We had a few spills and scraped knees, but this was mostly because we fell over each other trying to hang on.

He usually ignored us unless we got to rowdy, then he would shake his fist at us and tell us to clear off.

He was all hunched over and dirty and often smelled bad and we had no idea where he lived.

The Rag and Bone Men collected any unwanted household items or used clothing. He rode through the neighborhoods with his horse and cart shouting, "Ragand Bones", at the top of his voice. If someone had

A Rag and Bone Man

something, they wanted to get rid of he would either trade for a goldfish or a whiting stone.

Auntie Annie always said no to a goldfish, always trading for a whiting stone.

A whiting stone was made from a mixture of pulverized stone, cement, bleach powder and water. The mixture was ground up into a thick paste and then formed into a rectangular slab about the size of a bar of soap. It was used to make your front doorstep white.

My Auntie Annie always said you could tell how clean a house was on the inside by the whiteness of their doorstep.

Not all our friends were kids; one was Rita. She was an Alsatian, *(German Shepherd)*. She belonged to Bobby Dearden,

Rita was a remarkable animal. Never on a leash, never chained up, just another member of the gang and wherever Bobby went Rita would just tag along.

Kathleen Oakley had a dog too; his name was Rex. He was a little dog with a big temper and was always barking and nipping at our ankles so we wouldn't let him come with us when we went off to play.

On school nights we would just hang around the streets playing games, like kick the can, or just throw a ball up and down the street or bounce it off a wall. And once in a while get a game of cricket going with a stick and a ball.

On Saturdays or during a holiday we would often venture farther afield.

Laura and I would try and sneak out of the house before my Auntie Annie caught us. Not because she didn't want us to go play, but rather she wanted us to take Stella with us, which we did, reluctantly, more often than not.

Stella was only three and she couldn't keep up when we ran, and we would have to lift her over things. But she didn't cry when she fell down or tell on us when we did something we were not supposed to, so I guess it was okay.

One of our favorite places to play was the Farington Lodge woods.

We would walk down the lane and if the gate was open and nobody was watching we would run across the road and in through the gate. If the gate was closed, we wouldn't be able to go in on account of we had Stella, Rita, and if Tubby Trelfal was with us there was no way he was climbing over that wall.

Once inside we would go over to *'our den'*.

This was an area where they dumped stuff from the big house, like an old sink and bits of broken furniture and always lots of tires.

The tires would be stacked three or four high and sometimes even higher than that. We would play *'pretend,'* like, Cowboys and Indians or Soldiers at war and climb in the tires and pretend to shoot each other.

Now the Lodge had a Groundskeeper. He was a big man and he was always dressed the same. A tweed jacket with leather elbows and pants he tucked into his boots and he very often carried a shotgun over his arm, and always had a pipe sticking out of his mouth.

And he had a dog.

It was a fierce looking, white bulldog.

He never kept it on a lease, it just waddled alongside him. Probably because it had such short legs and was so fat it had a hard time keeping up.

Having Rita with us was always a good thing because when she sensed the Groundskeeper close, she would perk up her ears and give a low growl and we would all be off in a flash, well as fast as we could, hampered as we were by having to carry Stella. And Tubby Trelfal couldn't run very fast either.

Laura would pick Stella up under her arms and run as fast as she could, tripping and stumbling all the way. Out of the gate and across the street we would run and when the Groundskeeper and his dog reached the gate, they would just look at us and then turn back.

Now in hindsight I think it was just a great big game to that Groundskeeper because he never crossed the road, never shouted at us and never destroyed our den.

But one time things did sort of take a bad turn.

It was a Saturday and we were playing in the tires as usual. Laura had lifted Stella inside a stack. You could barely see her head over the top.

Now Rita loved to chase rabbits and when she saw one, well she was off in a flash.

I suppose we were preoccupied playing so we got no prior warning that the Groundskeeper and his dog were near.

When we saw him, we all panicked and took off running for the gate. But then we remembered Stella, she was still in the tires.

We shouted back at her to duck down and keep quiet and we would come back for her.

Rita saw us leaving and came running back but instead of following us she ran toward the tires where Stella was still hiding.

Rita started barking and jumping up and down and no amount of calling made her come. She was just not going to leave Stella behind.

All was lost. Not only were we going to lose Stella, we were going to lose Rita as well.

How on earth would we explain it to Auntie Annie if we came home without Stella?

But Rita was a smart dog. Suddenly she turned on that Bulldog and attacked it. It was the first time she had ever done that.

The Groundskeeper had no choice but to try and break them up. He picked up a stick and started hitting them as hard as he could, trying to get those two dogs apart.

There was snapping and snarling, and the fur was flying, and the Groundkeeper was shouting.

In the melee we saw the chance that Rita had given us, and yanking Stella out of the tires, we hightailed it out of there as fast as we could.

Once we got across the lane, we stopped, scared to death that Rita had been killed by that bulldog or worse got shot by the Groundskeeper. Plus, we were feeling pretty bad about abandoning her.

Bobby Deardon said he could never go home again on account of his dad would murder him for letting Rita get killed.

Then, here comes Rita running out of the woods, none the worse for wear.

We all petted her, and she just wagged her tail. Yes, she was a good dog to have around.

We didn't dare go back in those woods for a while. Well, at least not right away.

We had two more episodes with the Groundskeeper and his dog that summer.

Getting toward the end of August the apples in the lodge's orchard were beginning to ripen. We could see them over the wall from the field, just hanging on the trees.

So, one day we decided it would be a great idea to *'Raid'* the orchard.

We knew it was risky, but a lot was a stake, and those apples drew us like a magnet.

We would have to pass in front of the big house to get to the orchard and even though there were lots of trees to hide behind the chances of getting caught was high and a lot more dangerous than just playing in the tires.

There was about seven of us, including Rita and at the last minute, wouldn't you know it, we got stuck with Stella.

But the plans had already been made and nobody wanted to back out.

So off we went through the gate.

Hugging the wall furthest away from the Lodge we cautiously made our way on our apple stealing mission.

So far so good. We kept to the trees until we suddenly saw the prize ahead of us. Large, red, juicy apples dripping from the branches.

Throwing caution to the wind we all took off running at top speed towards those apple trees.

A few of us were better at climbing trees than others, so up we went. There was me, Bobby

Deardon, and a couple more kids and we scampered up until we could reach the apples.

Now being a girl, I always had on either a dress or a skirt and a couple of the boys on the ground started giggling, saying "We can see y'r knickers."

I shouted down, "If ya want some of these apples, you best shut y'r gob."

That quietened 'em down.

Grabbing what we could reach, we dropped them down to those below, all the while eating our fill, those below stuffing as many apples as they could in their pockets.

Kathleen Oakley had thought ahead and had brought her school bag and was quickly filling it up.

Suddenly Rita let out a low growl, and we all froze, and looking towards the house saw the Groundskeeper off in the distance running towards us shaking his fist. This time we had gone too far. He looked really angry.

We slid down the trees as fast as we could and headed for the wall, knowing that was our only means of escape.

A couple of us jumped up and made it to the top of the wall, giving a hand to the ones below who were not such good climbers.

Laura lifted Stella and one of the lads grabbed her by the hand and hoisted her up, then dropped her down on the other side where the rest were waiting to catch her. Other than a scraped knee she did okay. Thank god Tubby Trelfal was not with us because there was no way we could have handed him up!

By now everyone was either on the other side or still straggling the top of the wall; only one remained, Rita.

We just couldn't leave her behind again.

Bobby kept calling her name and urging her to jump up. She kept trying but all you could hear were her claws scraping the wall as she slid back down.

The Groundskeeper was getting closer, but he was greatly slowed down by his lumbering bulldog.

Suddenly Rita ran off in their direction, and we thought, oh no there's going to be another dog fight.

But Rita got halfway there, then suddenly turned on her heels and started running back towards us as fast as she could, and with a great leap landed on top of that wall and over the other side.

The rest of us quickly scampered down thanking our lucky stars that we had escaped and still had lots of apples.

Or so we thought. When the last of us landed on the other side somebody said, 'eh 'um."

Well as it just so happened on that warm sunny afternoon the Cricket Club had decided to have a game of cricket in the side field and unfortunately, we had just landed in the middle of it. What a sight we must have been. Seven scaggy looking kids and a dog just plopped right down there in the middle of their game.

Everybody stopped what they were doing and just stared at us.

So, with our backs literally against the wall, what else was there to do?

We just started ambling across the pitch like it was just another walk in the park. We didn't hurry. What was the point? We were all worn out anyway on account of our escape and we knew we were caught dead to rights.

Suddenly Billy Marsden broke ranks and running shouted, "Hey, look, I found a cricket ball."

Between clenched teeth Bobby Deardon said, "Ya stupid twit, put it down, that's their ball."

But then one of the players said, "Here, toss it over."

Which Billy did, then the cricket player tossed back the apple that Billy had accidently thrown instead of the ball and said, "Good toss lad, now throw me the ball."

A couple of us gave a weak smile and a little low three fingered wave to our audience and started off again across the field.

Then we heard someone start to laugh and before you know it, they were all laughing at us.

When we got back up to where the swings were, we just collapsed in the grass in peals of laughter and gorged ourselves on our hard-won apples.

We would have one more encounter with the Groundskeeper and his dog that summer.

One day while playing on the swings we heard a screeching of tires and a loud yelp.

We rushed over to the lane and there, laying in the road was that bulldog. Blood was coming out of his mouth.

A motor car was pulled over on the side of the road and the driver standing over him just staring down.

The bulldog attempted to move, and we could see that he was trying to drag himself off the road but only his front legs were working, his hind legs dragging behind him.

Then the Groundskeeper came up through the woods with his shot gun over his arm.

He went over to his bulldog and wiping tears off his face with the back of his hand raised that gun and shot his dog to death.

We were horrified, but for the first time ever that Groundskeeper spoke to us.

He said, "It was for't best. I had to put poor Caesar out 'is misery."

We finally learned what that bulldogs name was but now it was too late.

15

LEARNING TO FLY

Across the street from us lived the Duckworth's. They had one daughter and her name was Marjorie.

She was several years older than us, at least thirteen and she was the only teenager we knew.

We had no teen magazines or television to compare her with, so we always thought she was very grown up and glamourous, and we often pretended we were her.

She never played with us because she said, "You're just little kids." But we would hang around her every chance we got.

One day she made my sisters and I an offer that we just couldn't refuse. She said she'd teach us how to fly like the fairies. She would give us flying lessons. Of course, we believed her, she was thirteen and knew everything.

She charged us a penny a lesson.

Our first lesson started by jumping off the front gate because it was fairly low. She showed us how to hold our arms out and how to land.

When we had mastered that we graduated to the back gate which was much higher. I have to admit it was hard on the feet when you landed!

Our final lesson was from the top of the wall.

She told us when we mastered that, then we would be able to fly. But! and this was a very important *but*, you could only fly at midnight, this was the witching hour when the fairies were about.

Fairies are a big part of English folk lore. Fairies were little people with gossamer wings and pointed ears and lived at the bottom of every bodies garden and they were extremely mischievous.
 If one of us did something naughty we would often say we didn't do it and that it was probably the fairies from the bottom of our garden.
Every child grew up believing in them. It was like believing in Father Christmas or the Tooth Fairy.

Now it just so happened that Laura was in a school play called, '*A mid-summer nights dream*' and she was one of the fairies. Our Mother made her a fairy dress for the part.
Now that our flying lessons were complete, and Laura had a fairy dress we decided it was time to give it a try.
Laura wore her fairy dress to bed one night and when our parents came in to check on us on their way to bed, we pretended to be fast asleep.
 After they were in bed and all the lights were off, we laid awake until we were sure they were asleep. Then Laura crept downstairs to check the time.
Almost midnight.

We stood at the top of the stairs, Laura in her fairy dress holding her arms out like Marjorie had shown us, and then she went sailing off into mid-air.

Well, either the downstairs clock was wrong or she had failed her flying lessons miserably, because she landed half way down with a thump and then rolled the rest of the way to end up sprawled out at the bottom of the stairs.

Of course, all the racket woke up our Mother and Dad and when they saw Laura laying there at the bottom of the stairs, they ran down in horror to see if she was okay.

But she was just bruised with a big knot on her forehead.

My Dad turned to me and said, "What on earth happened?"

"She was trying to fly," I told him.

"Trying to what?"

"Fly. Marjorie's been giving us flying lessons, but I think the downstairs clock must be wrong. Is it midnight yet?" I asked.

"MIDNIGHT!!!"

They picked Laura up and checked her out, putting cold towels on her knees and the bump on her head, and carried her back to bed.

My Dad said to her, "If Marjorie Duckworth told you to jump off a cliff would you............" he stopped in mid-sentence, "Yes, I guess you would."

We were told not to associate with Marjorie anymore and not to listen to anymore of her tricks, and that he was going to have a talk with her mum and dad.

Marjorie got mad at us for telling because she got in trouble. She told Laura, "You probably did it all wrong. Serves you right for not paying proper attention to your lessons."

"Yea," we conceded; she was probably right. As time went on, we watched Marjorie grow up into a young lady.

She wore full skirts and a tight sweater which showed off her breasts. None of us had breasts and we couldn't wait to get some. When we took a bath, we would check to see if anything was growing on our chests. I thought it would never happen.

Laura got them first and I was green with envy.

Marjorie wore nylons and high heeled shoes and a scarf around her neck. All in all, she was our role model.

One morning we saw a man working on the Duckworth's garden wall. He was knocking down the old one and a truck delivered him a bunch of bricks to build a new wall.

Anything happening in the streets was interesting, so we ended up over there watching him work.

He would slap mortar on a brick and then put it in place, all the time a cigarette was hanging out of his mouth, smoke curling up into his eyes.

He was not very old, and we thought he was very good looking.

He didn't get mad when we pestered him with questions.

Us: "What you doin'?"

Him: "Building a wall."

Us "Why?"
Him: " 'cause the old one's was fallin' down."
Us: "Why?"
Him: " 'cause it was old. Don't you 'ave anythin' better do than 'ang around 'ere, asking all the questions?"
Us: "No."
Us: "Do ya like smokin'?"
Him: "Yea."
Us: "Why?"
Him: "'ere take a drag and find out for yourself?"

"Okay," said Laura. So, he passed over his cigarette.

Laura took a drag on it and coughed a bit, then she handed it to me. I took a drag on it and thought I would choke. I couldn't stop coughing, then I got lightheaded and woozy.

"Yuck," I said.

He just laughed.

We hung around him most of the day and probably made complete nuisances of ourselves. Soon some of the other kids came over and we told them we had taken a drag on his cigarette. Laura bragged it was great. I said it was great too, but Laura told everybody I had choked, and they all laughed at me.

In the afternoon we saw Marjorie get off the bus, she was coming home from work.

The workman whistled and said she looked smashing and we told him she lived here in this house.

When Marjorie came up, she smiled at the workman and he smiled back. Then he said to us, "Why don't you kids clear off?"

Reluctantly we walked away but watched them from across the street, we were all giggly and making fun of them.

Next day the workman was there again.

We asked him if he was in love with Marjorie and did he want to kiss her? He said, "She's a real good-looking tart." We guess that was what a lad called a girl when he really liked her.

They talked to each other every day when Marjorie came home from work. They smoked lots of cigarettes and kept smiling at each other and when Marjorie was there the workman didn't get any work done.

But then eventually the job was finished, and we didn't see him for a few days.

Then one Friday night we saw him go to her house. He was all dressed up. He knocked on her front door and when it opened, he went inside.

After a while they both came out and went off down the street to the bus stop. He was probably taking her to the pictures or something. Next time we saw Marjorie we asked her if she was going to go on another date with him.

She said no, that he'd got fresh, "You know how workmen are, always whistling and flirting with girls."

We said "yes", but we really didn't know what she meant.

16

THE KING IS DEAD, LONG LIVE THE QUEEN

In 1951 it was time for Stella to start *Infants*, she was four years old now, I was eight and Laura, who was ten was preparing for her 11+ (I will explain the 11+ later).

Things were easier for Stella when she started school.

She would walk to school with Laura and I and Auntie Annie would come to collect her at noon.

She got to play with other kids and have access to toys, coloring books and everything a kid could want.

In 1952 she started in Form 1, full time, then she walked both to and from school with us.

Having two sisters to watch out for her was a great asset and so she had an easier transition to full time school life than Laura and I had.

Nobody messed with those Rothwell girls.

About midmorning, during playtime on February 6th, 1952, the teacher came out and blowing her whistle to get everyone's attention, told us all to go in the Assembly Hall for an important announcement.

A lot of speculation was going around on just what had happened. You just didn't get called back into assembly unless something very ominous had occurred.

When we got inside and everybody had settled down, we were informed, by a very emotional Headmaster, that the King was dead, and that we were to be sent home early and did not have to attend school the next day for the national day of mourning.

Unfortunately, not realizing the gravity of the news we had just received, we all cheered at the prospect of an early day and one extra day off.

The Headmaster was appalled, and we were promptly silenced and told, in no uncertain terms that this was not a time to be celebrating but a time of deep sorrow for the whole country.

When we got home, because of the lack of communications, my Auntie Annie did not yet know King George had died.

I can remember the shocked look on her face when we told her, and she started wiping her eyes with her handkerchief.

We didn't have television or telephones and it would not be until the next day when the Daily Mail newspaper came out before we knew the details.

Our celebration at having the day off school was soon crushed as we were not allowed to go out and play in the street as it would be considered disrespectful.

My mother bought my Dad a black tie and material to make a black armband, and for the next twenty-four hours all curtains were drawn, all across the country, in respect for the deceased monarch.

King George VI had been a popular king, more than likely because, since he was not the *Heir Apparent,* he had not been raised or groomed for such a position and was a more down to earth person than previous monarchs.

He had become heir to the throne quite unexpectedly following the sudden abdication of his brother, Prince Edward, who did so in order to marry American socialite Wallis Simpson.

The new King George VI was now thrust into the head of a country embroiled in World War I and, to make matters worse for the shy young man he also had a debilitating stutter, but this seemed only to endear him more to the British people and his popularity grew.

He became an important symbolic leader for the British people.

Unfortunately, the stress of years at war took a toll on King George VI, and his health began to seriously decline. He died of lung cancer when he was just fifty-six years old after only twenty-six years on the throne.

It was at the exact time of his death that Princess Elizabeth, his presumptive heir, was given the daunting task of taking over his royal duties.

She was only 25 years old when she became ruler of the British commonwealth.

Originally, she had only been third in line for the throne and under normal circumstances would not have been expected ever to become queen.

But when her uncle, Prince Edward, abdicated, it automatically made her next in line after her father.

When she came to the throne, she had already been married for four years and had two children, Charles born in 1948 and Anne 1950.

During her reign she had two more children, Andrew in 1960 and Edward in 1964.

The very second her father died she became Queen. Hence the phrase. *The King is dead, long live the Queen.*

Even though she immediately became Queen upon his death, she would not be crowned until the following year and so on June 3rd, 1953 with the year of mourning over, the whole county prepared for her coronation.

It was now a time for celebration.

The Streets prepared.

We tied crepe paper buntings from the lamposts and set tables down the middle of the street in preparation.

And our Mother and Dad thought this was a good time to purchase that new contraption the Television they had been hearing about.

It had been announced earlier in the year that the crowning of the Queen would be televised, and the sales of televisions skyrocketed.

This was the first time ever that ordinary people were going to be able to watch a monarch's coronation in their own homes.

The television was a small, bulky affair with a picture in black and white. Color television had not been invented yet, but to us the black and white picture television was a marvel.

We were the envy of the neighborhood. There was only one other family that I knew of who owned a television and they lived in a posh house down the lane.

The only problem on the actual day of the coronation was the typical English weather, it poured with rain!

But that didn't stop us. People all over the country was holding parties in the decorated streets of their towns and cities, and in London the roads were packed with people waiting to see the procession that would take place. And much to the credit of the new Queen, when she left Westminster Abbey, she insisted on riding through the streets of London in an open carriage in spite of the rain.

There had been a lot of controversy in the Government as to whether it would be *'right and proper'* to televise such a solemn occasion.

Several members of the Cabinet at the time, including Sir Winston Churchill, urged the Queen not to have the ceremony televised.

But the Queen received this suggestion coldly and refused to listen to their protests.

She had made her decision!

And in a move that endeared her even more to her subjects, she announced that nothing would stand between her people's right to participate in the occasion.

So, on June 2nd, 1953 at 11 o'clock, all over the country, people settled down in front of their television sets to watch the crowning of Queen Elizabeth II.

Because we were the only house in the neighborhood with a television set, my Mother and Dad invited all who wanted to could come and watch it on our television.

Now when you entered our front door, on the left was the staircase, the one where Laura had taken her first flight as a fairy, which led to the bedrooms upstairs and to the right a narrow hallway that led to the kitchen in back. Another door to the right of the hallway opened into the dining and living room area, which was one large room. A big bay window overlooked the garden in front, and a large picture window overlooked the yard in back.

They moved most of the furniture against the walls and invited the neighbors to bring their own chairs and they lined them all up in rows.

My Dad raised the television as high as he could so those in the back could get a good look.

The younger ones sat cross legged on the floor down in front.

Laura far right, me with a ribbon in my hair, Bobby Deardon front & center

For the next few hours the grownups sat glued to that television. Of course, we got bored in just a short while and it wasn't long before we were off outside.

After the ceremony was over, thankfully, there was a break in the weather and the food and drinks were brought out and we all celebrated.

Television had hit our lives and changed it forever.

Television had come to northern England in 1951 but very few people had a television set.

BBC was the only station and that was mostly news and documentaries.

The BBC's monopoly on English television came to an end in 1955 when the new independent, ITV began broadcasting and we saw television commercials for the first time.

By now just about every family had a television set.

Along with the move into commercial television came competition, both stations vying for the same audience and *Children's Hour* was now broadcast on BBC from 5 pm to 6 pm every day of the week, with the biggest audience being on the weekends when parents joined in.

Children's classic characters like Bill and Ben the flower pot men and Andy Pandy soon became all the rage.

Bill and Ben, the Flowerpot Men.   *Andy Pandy*

It was the time of day during the week when children could be expected to be home from school and was aimed at an audience aged from five to fifteen.

The time would eventually come when kids wouldn't go out and play as much after school but watch television instead.

Conversation would cease, and instead of sitting around the fire in the evening, families all over England would be sitting round the television set.

But still, programing was limited, and it would be several years before we felt the real impact television would have on the world.

A few months after the coronation, after we had gone back to school, the Queen went on a grand tour, crisscrossing England in her special train.

Since the train would be travelling through Leyland and Farington, the whole school went down to the tracks to watch it pass by.

With the younger kids out in front we marched down the street two by two then through a field down to the railway tracks where the train was due to travel.

We had all been given a small Union Jack to wave at the Queen.

We lined up against the fence, four and five deep and waited.

When the train came flying past, we all raised our little flags and waved at the passing train.

The train, which was just seven coaches long was past us in a less than a minute but several of us claimed we had seen the Queen looking out of the window and she had waved back at us, which was highly unlikely, but it gave us a good story to tell our parents.

Then we were marched back to school again to continue on with the day's lessons.

I imagine the same scene took place all across the country.

17

GUY FAWKES DAY/BONFIRE NIGHT

Guy Fawkes was one of a group of conspirators who on November the 5th 1605, plotted to blow up the Houses of Parliament while King James 1st was inside. A day that was set for the King to open Parliament.

The plan, known as the *"Gunpowder Plot,"* was discovered the day before, when Guy Fawkes was found with thirty-six barrels of gunpowder in the cellar below the Houses of Parliament with matches in his pocket.

Because the plot was foiled, instead of The Houses of Parliament burning and the King being blown to bits, the people lit Bonfires all over England to celebrate his safety.

This is known as Guy Fawkes Day or, Bonfire Night, and has been observed every year since then, all over England on November 5th by lighting a bonfire and burning Guy Fawkes in effigy.

Weeks before Bonfire night we would spend every spare minute collecting firewood. Daily trips to Farington Lodge Woods would net us a fair haul, and on most days, you could see us coming out of the woods dragging branches, logs, anything we could carry that would burn.

The Groundskeeper turning a blind eye to our thievery. He was probably glad to get rid of all that dead wood lying about.

We would even drag out the occasional tire, but if any grownups saw one in the bonfire, they would make us take it out.

Kids in every neighborhood would be doing the same thing and if we ran into another gang in the woods there would often be a scuffle.

Building the Bonfire

It wasn't any advantage having Rita because she knew all the kids in the neighborhood, and she would just wag her tail when she saw them.

We built our bonfire in the back field, just up from our house. When we went wood scavenging, we would leave someone behind to stand guard because it was not uncommon to be raided and have our wood stolen.

So, when we piled up the wood we would try and leave a space in the middle to hide in, to catch someone in the act.

Of course, the other gangs weren't the only ones stealing other kids wood. We would also go on raids to neighboring bonfires.

A few streets down from us the kids who lived there were building their own bonfire and we always tried to outdo each other.

This particular day we decided to go and raid their bonfire.

The raiding party consisted of about four lads and three of us girls.

We decided to leave Stella on guard because all she had to do was sit in the middle of the bonfire and holler at the top of her lungs if someone came and then we would all come running.

Stella was okay with this arrangement, she never argued, she just did as she was told. I think she was just chuffed to be included, because she was just a little kid and we were much older!

Off we went up the back field, across the top field through the farmers field until we came to the rival's streets.

So far so good. We crept down between the houses and right down to their bonfire.

Nobody in sight.

Looking inside, nobody there either, so we started grabbing as many branches as we could.

Suddenly there was a piercing scream. It was Stella.

We dropped the branches, and all took off running as fast as we could, back to our bonfire.

When we came across the field, we could see Stella surrounded by the rival gang still screaming her head off.

Some of the kids were pulling branches off our bonfire, but when they saw us running towards them, hollering all the way, they just stopped what they were doing and stared at us, ready for a fight.

When we got there, we just faced off. Both sides caught in the act. They knew what we had been up to.

"Get away from our fire," Billy Marsden said menacingly.

"I'll set Rita on ya," said Bobby Deardon.

Rita just wagged her tail and lick a few hands.

"Oh yea, go on then."

Then we all just kind of stood there looking at each other.

It was then suggested that both sides proclaim a truce and leave each other's bonfire alone.

It was agreed.

We never did raid their bonfire again and as far as we could tell they left ours alone too.

Although, ours was much bigger than theirs, way bigger.

Another part of Guy Fawkes Day or Bonfire night was making a scarecrow-like image out of old clothes stuffed with grass or straw and we called it *'The Guy,'* to represent the conspirator Guy Fawkes.

After we made *'The Guy,'* which was usually a week or so before the 5th, we would take him around our Streets and ask people for, *'A penny for the Guy.'* Then we would use the money we collected to buy fireworks and sparklers for the big night.

As bizarre as this may sound it's not unlike kids today dressing up like monsters going around asking for candy on Halloween.

On Bonfire night the adults would supervise the lighting of the bonfire.

Before the fire was lit someone would throw *'The Guy'* on top of the pile and when the fire roared to life, we would all wait for him to catch on fire, then we would all cheer.

This burning of Guy Fawkes in effigy commemorated the capture, torture, and burning of the real Guy Fawkes.
How about that for a kid's bedtime story!

Barbaric as it sounds, the true meaning of Guy Fawkes Day is lost in time and now it's just a night of fun and fireworks.
Earlier in the day, before the fire was lit, we would take potatoes and scratch our initials in the skin and put them under the branches.
After the fire burned down and all the fireworks and sparklers were done, we would rake through the embers and find our potato and after scaping of the burned skin sit around the fire and enjoy a piping hot potato.

18

BLACKBERRY PIE

Sundays were the best day of the week, especially in the summertime, where one day could bring you the most glorious weather, with rare cloudless blue skies and warm temperatures.

England is a country of wild flowers and bushes. Rhododendrons and Hydrangeas can grow to amazing heights, covered in every color imaginable.

And fields, carpeted with the small English Daisies, and the brilliant purple Thistle whose seeds would be food for the birds in Autumn.

Elderberries, Raspberries and my favorite, Blackberries also grew in wild abundance, ours for the picking.

Sunday was a day of rest throughout the country.

All the shops and markets were closed, and the pubs were only allowed to be open for five hours.

This was a family day and our Mother and Dad would take us on outings, like blackberry picking or to beach at Southport, or once in a while a trip to Wigan to visit with family.

Blackberry picking was great fun and my favorite.

My Dad would take along a walking stick so he could hook the branches to bring them closer for us to reach, and we ate just about as many as we put in our baskets and they didn't care, and our tongues and lips would be all colored purple.

And we all knew the very next day Auntie Annie would bake a delicious Blackberry pie.

We walked along the hedgerow and would see all kinds of songbirds and try and identify them. My Mother knew just about the names of all we saw.

There were always lots of rabbits and once in a while we would see a hedgehog or a badger.

The hedgehog would roll itself up into an impenetrable ball when disturbed, but my Dad steered us clear of the badger because they were not quite so timid and could be dangerous if threatened. It was also not unusual to see a red fox.

Once when we were blackberry picking, we saw a herd of sheep coming down the lane with two sheep dogs trailing behind them nipping at their hoofs, keeping them on the move. No need for a farmer, the dogs could do all the work.

My Dad said they were probably leading the herd from one field to another for grazing, or perhaps back to their pen at the farm.

Many farmers would paint his initials on the side of his sheep so he could tell which were his in case the flocks got mixed up.

Now one of these sheep had EB painted on its side, different initials from the rest of the flock. When asked, my Dad told us it was the sheep's name. Elsie Baa-lamb. He was so funny. He was always saying silly things like that.

Like, if we came home from school with a really good tale, he would look down at you and listen to every word you said. Then with his hands on his hips and surprise in his voice he would say, "Well, I never, I'll go ta' foot of our stairs."

Another funny thing he used to say if we came in and our Mother wasn't at home, like maybe she had just run down to the grocery shop and we would say, "Where's mi Mum?" he'd say, "She ran off wit' postman." He was so funny; it was great having a Dad.

One day when we were out blackberry picking, we came across a Gypsy camp.

There were many Gypsy's wandering around England in those days, but this was the first time I had seen them this close up.

They were just sitting around, probably enjoying the warm day as we were. We looked at them and they looked at us. Then we just went on minding our own business.

Gypsy Camp

Sometimes when they were coming down the lane you could hear them before you saw them because they had pots and pans and all sorts of gear hanging from the sides of their caravan. And you could hear the clip, clop of their horse's hooves on the road.

Gypsy's were nomads and could originate from almost anywhere.

Romania is most commonly thought of to be their place of origin but history shows that even though they seemed to follow a common lifestyle most Gypsies were in no way related and could come from many different parts of the world and wandered through every country in Europe, recognizing no boarders.

Some were of Irish decent and they were called Traveler's, but mostly they came from Europe and like most groups that lived outside of society they were greatly persecuted, especially by the Nazi's during the war who decimated half of their population.

They had no written laws or written history and at that time their children didn't go to school and though they spoke the language of the country they roamed in; it was in a distinct dialect that was hard to understand.

They would appear one day and just settle in for about a month or so and then move on.

That was probably about as much time that it took for the local populous to get them on the move again.

The men would do odd jobs, and sometimes the whole family would work a farmer's field, much like todays itinerant farm workers. And sometimes the young women would go into town in their colorful traditional costumes and dance and draw a crowd who would throw them a few coins.

Their caravans were colorfully painted with intricately carved design's and could fetch a good price on today's market.

But, having no running water or sewer facilities their camps soon became unlivable and it was time to move on to a new site.

We were always told not to talk or go near them as they were said to have a propensity to steal children.

Sometimes if we misbehaved our parents would say they were going to give us to the Gypsy's.

Having that being said, we really had no idea what kind of people they were. They were probably very misunderstood.

They were a close-knit prideful group and lived a way of life that their ancestors had done for generations.

And although the English Gypsy's lifestyle of today has probably drastically changed, they have a lasting place in history. I have no idea of the laws governing them or if they even still roam the English country-side.

Another of our favorite outings was going to the seaside at Southport. Most people who went to the seaside had to go on the train but since we had a car, we got to drive there.

We would take sandwiches and drinks and towels, blankets and deck chairs, and a stroller for Stella and everything would fit in the car.

And best of all, when we got there, they would buy us an ice cream cone or an ice lollie.

We got the treat before we went on the beach so we wouldn't get sand on them.

They would buy us buckets and spades to build sandcastles with and pinwheels that would spin in the wind.

Southport beach is on such a slight incline that the distance between high and low tide could be, at times, at least three-quarters of a mile, and at low tide coral reefs would be visible and exposed to the sun.

So, when we went to Southport there was a good possibility that we would get nowhere near the sea.

But when the tide started coming back in, it could cover that three-quarter mile in a matter of half an hour.

But we didn't mind if the tide was out, our main focus was building sandcastles and even if the tide was reachable, the water was so cold you couldn't stand to even put your toes in.

My Mother and Dad would sit in their deck chairs and relax in the sunshine while we played in the sand.

We would get there early in the morning and spend the whole day.

Walking along the beach searching for shells and crabs or building sandcastles and digging

108

holes to reach the water which always lurked just below the surface.

It was usually quite chilly, even if the sun was shining, as a breeze always blew the cool air off the Atlantic. But we didn't mind, we were used to cool weather.

By noon we would have our lunch, which we had brought from home. And by one in the afternoon, if the weather stayed nice, the beach would be packed with people.

Southport Beach

19

SISTERS

The further away we got from the war the happier people were. It seemed sunnier, warmer, people were friendlier and said "hello" on the street, and smiled more.

Auntie Annie looked happier too, and we didn't seem to be as much underfoot as usual.

And the nightmares were melting away.

Our school holiday that summer was the best ever.

Sometimes it was just us three sisters.

That's the best part of having sisters, you were never alone, we were just part of each other.

Every day I knew they were going to be there. There was always someone to play with.

We would go outside to play, not really knowing what we were going to do or where we were going to go, it didn't matter. Just wandering about. It was great to wander. I feel sad for the children of today that wandering isn't a part of their lives.

No plans needed. We just drifted along, one minute not doing anything and then doing something.

Wandering across to the park or deciding to go on a picnic.

"Let's go down to the pond at Clayton Bottoms."

"Why don't we take some jam butties." Meandering the whole way there. Stopping to look at a shiny stone, follow a frog, pick up a walking stick.

Warm and sunny days, no hurry. We might see a dragonfly along the way and when we arrived at the pond, there were hundreds, millions of them just flitting across the surface of the water.

The pond, half hidden by reeds and a few rocks, and tiny fish that darted back and forth and big jelly globs of tadpoles that floated on the surface or hung on the reeds.

We sat on the grass beneath the *'magic-far way-tree'* to eat our jam butties. That old oak tree was a longstanding friend, its leaf laden branches canopied the pond and reached up into the clouds.

In its middle was a big hole, enough to fit one little girl in at a time.

When you crawled inside, it smelled of damp wood and worms, and if you tilted your head back you could look up through its decaying center and see the sky way at the top.

We would take turns looking up to see if we could see any fairies. You see, at the top of that tree, high in the clouds, was a *'magic faraway land*, where the sun was always shining and candy hung from tree branches like acorns, and rabbits could talk and beautiful birds landed on your hand and little fairy houses where the fairies lived. Our imaginations ran wild.

The thing I hated most was, as girls we were expected to wear dresses or skirts, every little girl did. No girls ever wore pants even when out playing.

Now I must admit, as a child I would rather climb a tree or catch a frog, or wade in the water to catch tadpoles than pick daisies or play house with dolls. That dress always got in my way. The solution? Tuck my skirt in my knickers.

But once in a while I would go home and forget to untuck it and Auntie Annie would just have a fit. She'd say, "Have you no shame, letting everybody see your knickers?"

And Auntie Annie told my Mother that something had to be done about me.

So, one day when my Mother and Dad came home from the Market, she brought us each a pair of Dungarees.

She said, "All the girls in Preston are wearing them. I suppose it would do no harm for you to start wearing them." Problem solved.

Stella and I in our first pair of Jeans

At first the neighbors thought this was scandalous.

"Those Rothwell girls, always running wild!"

Mothers were appalled.

112

"What is this world coming to?"

"I knew those girls were trouble."

But before the end of the summer most girls were wearing them. I guess we were trendsetters.

20

FAIRIES

On one of our wanderings we found a really big, fat, green caterpillar. We had never seen anything like it before and we were not sure what it was.

It was decided we would take it to the Post Office. "Why on earth would you take it to the Post Office?" you might well ask. Well, because the lady at the Post Office wears a uniform and everybody knows that people who wear uniforms know everything, and she most likely would be able to tell us what it was.

So, we wrapped it up in a big leaf and off we went to the Post Office.

When we got there, the Post Office lady was standing behind her counter. She was pretty old with curly hair and a pair of glasses that seemed to balance on the tip of her nose. I bet she was at least forty if she was a day. She had been at the Post Office for a very long time.

When we walked in, she looked down at us through her glasses and asked us what she could do for us. She was very pleasant.

Laura reached into her pocket and pulled out the caterpillar all wrapped up in the leaf and laid it on the counter and asked the Post Office lady if she could tell us what it was.

Well, she scrutinized it for a while then said, "Just wait 'ere a minute. I'll go in't back room and get my big book of information."

When she came back out another Post Office lady was with her. She was carrying a really big book.

She put it on the counter with a bang and opened it up.

Wetting her finger, she started leafing through the pages, scrutinizing each one, and saying to the other lady, "Um, do ya think it's one of them?" "Na, I don't think so," the other replied.

Then tapping her finger on one of the pages she declared, "There it is, I do believe it's one of them."

Now that counter was very high and we couldn't see what she was pointing at, but we could tell by the look on her face that she had found it, whatever *'it'* was.

The other lady leaned over for a closer look and declared, "I do believe y'r right."

Then they both looked over the counter at us and the one Post Office lady said, "Girls, we have ascertained, me and my friend Gladys 'ere, that what you 'ave is a real, genuine Fairy Elephant."

"Are you sure?" we replied in disbelief.

"Yep," she said, pointing back at the open page, "I'm sure of it. It says so right 'ere in this 'ere book of information."

Well, when we found out we had a real, genuine 'Fairy Elephant', we were really excited, and asked her what did she think we should do with it.

"Why take it 'ome 'a course and put it at the bottom of y'r garden and the fairies will come along tonight and take it back to where it belongs."

So that's what we did and sure enough the next morning that *'Fairy Elephant'* was gone.

Although for the next few weeks my Dad noticed that a lot of the leaves on this prize roses were all eaten up.

I have to give it to those two Post Office ladies, they never cracked a smile, but I'm sure, after we left, they had a really good laugh.

I don't think my Dad ever found out where that big, voracious, green caterpillar had come from.

We were so sure of the existence of fairies that we would put a little car on one side of our dresser at night and leave a note saying, 'fairy rides, one for a penny.'

My Dad told us we should only put the car out once in a while or else the fairies would get fed up and stop coming.

When we did leave the car out, we would try and stay awake to catch them in the act, but we never could.

But sure enough, the next morning that little car would be on the other side of the dresser and three pennies would be left there.

My Dad would give us a ration stamp and off we would go the next morning and buy a penny lollipop each.

21

THE TRAMP

More often than not when we went out to play, all the kids in the Streets would be there and you never knew where the day would lead us.

"Let's go down to the old reservoir," someone suggested.

As usual Auntie Annie had caught us on the way out and made us take Stella with us.

Auntie Annie never asked us where we were off to.

Stella was a bit older now, nearly four and was better at keeping up.

We knew we were not supposed to go down to the reservoir. Not only was it, *'No Trespassing,'* but it was also dangerous as the reservoir was deep and we were told often enough that someone might drown.

It was fenced off with an old broken-down wire fence which wasn't all that hard to get through and even Stella, Rita and Tubby Trelfal could easily get in.

Once inside we would skip stones in the water and see who could throw the furthest. Or try and catch minnows or tadpoles that swam there in abundance.

Most of the time nobody knew we were there but once in a while a man would come out of the old factory. Probably the caretaker and he would shake his fist at us and tell us to clear off.

He always threatened to tell our Dads, but he never did. Once he had gone back inside, we would just go back to what we were doing.

On this particular day, as we ambled around the edge of the reservoir, skimming stones across the surface, we noticed a white thread of smoke winding its way up through the trees.

Curious, we followed the smoke to see where it was coming from.

As we came through the trees, we saw a man sitting on a log in front of a fire, a pan of steaming hot water sending vapors into the air.

He was holding a tin cup in his hand and when he saw us coming out of the trees, he raised it in greeting, along with a nod and a grin.

He was dressed in old worn out clothes and his beard were long and grizzly, his teeth crooked and brown. He had a hat pulled low over his eyes with scraggly grey hair sticking out from underneath.

On the ground at his side was a knapsack and hanging between two trees was an old blanket tied on both ends like a hammock.

He didn't say anything at first, so we just ambled over, a couple of the lads sitting on the log next to him.

He was kind of dirty and a little bit smelly, but he seemed harmless enough.

"What you kid's up to then," he asked.

"Just playin," we told him.

"I th'ught nobodies supposed ta be in 'ere. It's dangerous ya know," he replied.

"Well y'r in 'ere, ain't ya," we said.

"I knows I am, but I'm a grown up, ain't I?"

Then he said, to no one in particular, "Is that y'r dog?" pointing at Rita, "Does it bite?" "That's Rita, and she only bites when I tell 'er to," Bobby Deardon replied.

The man called Rita over, but Rita wasn't having any of it and kept her distance.

"What ya doing 'ere? Were ya going?" we asked him.

"Anywhere the wind blows me," he said, "you wouldn't 'appen to 'ave a biscuit or anythin' else ta eat, would ya?"

"Na. What's that blanket fo'?"

"That's where I sleeps."

"Whys it 'anging from them trees."

"'cause if it starts rainin' I'll be off the ground, won't I? Would 'tha like a swing in it?" Of course, we jumped at the chance.

" 'ere 'old y'r 'orses," he said as the lads rushed forward, "let's give the girls a chance first."

So, he put three of us in at a time and swung us back and forth until we were dizzy.

Then he gave the lads a swing as well and we all had a good laugh.

After we'd had enough, we told him we had to go home now but could we come back tomorrow.

"Ok," he said, "but when ya comes back try and bring mi som'at ta eat will ya?"

So, we all agreed we would come back again the next day.

Early the next morning Kathleen Oakley came knocking at the door asking us if we were ready to go. She had a couple of biscuits in her hand.

As we started out the door my Dad said, "'ang on a minute, ready to go where? Just where are you off to in such a 'urry?"

We didn't want to say because we knew we would get in trouble for going down to the reservoir, but our Dad wasn't so easy to lie too; he could always see through us and I think he knew we were up to something and then he said, "Come on out wi' it."

So, we told him about the man and his hammock.

Well our Dad had a fit and grabbing his strap from off the wall march off down that field, with us all traipsing along behind him trying to keep up.

When that man saw my Dad heading down the field towards him with all of us in tow, he started picking up his stuff and hurried off leaving half of it behind.

But our Dad was too fast for him and jumping over the fence caught him by the scruff of his neck and all his kit went flying everywhere.

We had never seen anything like it and I never knew my Dad could move like that.

We were also a little relieved that his anger was directed at the man instead of us for going down to the reservoir in the first place.

We thought there was going to be a fight, but the man said, "I meant no 'arm governor, I'll just be on mi way and promise not to come back."

My Dad let him go and the man hurried off.

As we headed back up the field, we thought we were in the clear but then our Dad said, "'ow many times 'ave I got to tell you not to talk to strange men." *Thwack,* one, two, three! that strap came down across our bums, "and didn't I tell ya to stay away from that reservoir." *Thwack!*

Thwack! Thwack! we each got another.

It was a long time before we went down to that reservoir again.

But like most kids would, after a while we did. But we never did see that man again.

Now, looking back I don't think that tramp had any ill intent. I can honestly say he never touched any one of us inappropriately.

That's not saying he might not have if we had continued to go down there, but I really think he was just after something to eat. But I can also fully understand why my Dad was so upset.

22

ILL INTENT

Speaking of ill intent, Stella and I did have two episodes concerning men with ill intent and even though I was going to let them pass I decided to relate them here.

The first incident occurred one Saturday. Stella and I had gone to the Preston Market with our parents; I am not quite sure how old we were at the time.

I do remember it was bitterly cold and rainy and business was slow.

Our parents said we could go to the pictures (*movies*) in the afternoon.

They gave us a couple of shillings and off we went.

It was a short walk to the theater. When we got there the picture that was showing was *Moby Dick*.

We went to get our tickets and the lady told us the picture was already halfway through, but we could still go in if we wanted for half price.

Fair enough. So, we decided we would watch what was left. It beat standing in the cold at the shoe stall.

Usually when you went to the pictures an usher with a flashlight would show you to your seat. But he was sitting down smoking a cigarette and told us just to go on in and sit anywhere we wanted.

When we got inside, we had to wait a minute so our eyes could get accustomed to the dark. Then we made our way about halfway down and sat in the middle of the row.

Since it was the middle of the afternoon only about four or five people were in there, all sitting randomly around the theater.

After a while a man came down the row towards us. He was carrying his raincoat over his arm and flat cap in his hand and he sat down right next to Stella.

I was really engrossed in the movie and though it was strange that he would sit next to us when there were lots of empty seats, at the time I thought little of it.

Then Stella nudged me and said that the man kept touching her leg. I looked at him and he was just sitting there looking at the screen.

But, to make Stella feel better, I said let's just move down a bit, which we did. Next thing I know the man moved down also and sat right next to Stella again. I looked around for the usher, but he was nowhere to be seen.

I was not sure what to do. Stella was getting very upset. Should I shout at the man and tell him to leave her alone? But he was a grown up and I was a little afraid to say anything.

When I saw his hand come over to Stella's leg again, I hurriedly took her hand and pulled her out of her seat, and we headed for the curtain that would lead us out into the lobby. As we went through the curtain, I turned around and saw him heading up the aisle behind us.

Nobody was in the lobby, the usher nowhere to be seen.

We ducked into the lady's toilet. Peeking out of the door we could see him through the front window standing outside looking up and down the street.

We waited and after a while we saw him walking away.

We hurried out and ran all the way back to the Market. I told my Mother and Dad what had happened, and they commended me for doing the right thing.

The second incident occurred a few years later. I don't want to get to far ahead of my story, but we eventually moved away from Farington to a place called Orrell.

One warm sunny day, while exploring our new surroundings, Stella and I came across a small pond.

It sat a little off the road with a dirt path running parallel with it. The pond was separated from the path by about three feet of weeds and spindly little trees.

The pond itself had the ominous name of 'Dead Dog.' I suppose sometime in the past someone had found a dead dog there and the name had stuck.

Now Dead Dog was more of a bog than a pond. It had a few scraggly weeds around the perimeter and was covered in an algae that is commonly known in England as '*Ginny Green Teeth.*'

You couldn't get too close to the water because it was very muddy around the edges and we were afraid we would sink in. So, we just continued on along the path to see what else we could see.

The path was not long and ended at a farmer's gate. On the way there a man on a bicycle came riding towards us. He had probably gone down to the end and was going back the way he had come. He nodded at us when he passed.

When we reached the gate, we decided to go back as there was not much there to see or do.

Halfway back we could see the man's bike propped up against one of the trees next to the path.

We didn't think much of it, surmising he was down by the pond looking around.

As we got closer to the bike a movement in the trees by the pond caught our attention.

Looking over we saw the man standing there exposing himself.

At first, we just stood there in shock not sure what to do.

When I realized what he was doing I shouted, "You're a dirty old man! I'm telling my dad," and we started running towards the road.

As we went past his bike, I grabbed it by the handlebars and pushed it right in to Dead Dog. It stood upright for a second or two in the mud then tipped over into the water, disappearing from sight under all that *'Ginny Green Teeth,'* then we ran for the road as fast as we could.

The man came running out of hiding shaking his fist at us and shouting after us calling us brats, his white flabby thing flapping from side to side against his legs.

We could not believe the nerve of him getting mad at us after what he was up to!

23

JAM TARTS

Well back to my story.

Our Mother and Dad usually went to bed about ten o'clock and many nights we were still awake when they came up the stairs.

On this particular night Laura and I lay awake long after they had gone to bed. Stella was sleeping soundly,

It was decided, between the two of us, that we would sneak downstairs and, why not bake some jam tarts.

So, we waited a while to make sure they were asleep and then tip-toed down the stairs as quietly as we could. Then shutting the hallway door behind us turned on the light.

Going to the pantry, where they kept all the food, we got down the bag of flour, our little tin pie pans, some jam and oh yes, we needed sugar.

We used a chair to reach a mixing bowl and carried it over to the table like we saw Auntie Annie and Grandma Rothwell do.

How hard could it be.

Laura opened the bag of flour and tipped it into the bowl. But flour doesn't pour easily, and it came out in a big clump. Puff, down into that bowl, flour flying everywhere, on the table, on the floor, our faces and hair colored white.

We looked at each other with a gasp but when I saw Laura all covered with flour I started to laugh, she looked so funny.

"Shut up," she said, hardly being able to contain her own laughter, "you'll wake everybody up."

So, we scooped up what flour we could and proceeded.

Next, we needed some water, so Laura sent me off to bring a cup full. Then we dumped it in the bowl with the flour and she put her hands in to mix it all up.

Her fingers kept sticking together.

"We'll have to put more flour in," said Laura. So I grabbed the bag of flour and put more in.

Then we heard the hallway door opening, we froze. And turning towards it saw our Mother and Dad standing there.

What a sight we must have been.

My Dad yelled, "What on earth are you two doing?"

As my Mother cleaned us up my Dad started to work on the kitchen.

Then we just stood there waiting for our punishment. I was getting really tired, but they made us stand there until it was all cleaned up.

Then my Dad took down that strap and walked over to the bottom of the stairs and said, "Right, get over 'ere and 'old out your 'ands, then up to bed with you both and I don't want to 'ear another peep out of either one of you. Do you understand?"

We both nodded in unison and held out our hands.

Laura got it first and she screamed and hollered and then it was my turn, but when it came down it wasn't really that hard, but then Laura gave me that look so I started crying too.

As we were going back upstairs, clean pajamas and all, I whispered to Laura, "Did yours really 'urt that bad?" and she said "No, but just keep on crying."

We climbed into bed then heard my Mother and Dad come upstairs. And I swear to this day I heard them laughing.

24

THE CRAZY LADY UP THE STREET

Up the street from us lived a crazy old lady who never came out of her house. She always had her curtains pulled closed but once in a while we would see her peeking out from behind them.

Her garden was all overgrown and we used to sneak in on a dare and knock on her door and then run.

She was quite scary, and we made up all sorts of senecios about her.

Like, maybe she was a witch and if she caught one of us, she would keep us in a cage and fatten us up so she could have us for her supper.

We all knew the tale of Hansel and Gretel.

Or maybe she had killed someone, and their body was still somewhere in that house.

When my Dad found out what we had been doing he was really mad.

He came out and sat us all down, the three of us and all our friends too.

He told us we should be kind to her because she too had been in the war. He said she had been a nurse overseas and that she was shell shocked. I thought that meant that the Germans had thrown shells at her and thought that didn't seem bad enough to make her stay in her house all the time.

But then he explained that the shells were bombs and that they would be going off all the time and soldiers were getting blown up and if they weren't dead, they would take them to a hospital that was in a tent and the nurses would try and put them back together again. He said it was a really bad time and very scary and the nurses never knew if a bomb was going to drop on them too. He said she was affected by bad memories and that we should be kind to her.

Then he went and got all his gardening tools and the dust bin and broom and made us all start cleaning up her garden both back and front.

My Dad trimmed her hedges and we pulled weeds and swept her pathway.

When we had finished and were about to leave, we saw the front door open ever so slightly, we jumped back a bit not quite sure what to expect. We were not thoroughly convinced she wasn't a witch and maybe this was just a trick to catch one of us for her supper.

But then a hand came out and put a plate of biscuits on the doorstep.

My Dad stepped forward, but she closed it again before he had a chance to talk to her.

We felt pretty bad that we had bothered her so much, I guess she wasn't a witch after all.

We never did bother her again.

Although once in a while my Dad gathered us all together and we would go up and do her garden.

And always when we finished, out would come that plate of biscuits.

I am not sure if we willingly did her garden because we understood and sympathized with her or whether it was because we got a plate of biscuits in return. I like to think it was sympathy.

25

UP ON THE ROOF

I think from time immemorial kids have fought going to bed. My sisters and I were no exception. I found it a very frustrating part of my young years being sent to bed so early.

Each night we would beg to stay out a little longer or stay up a little later but to no avail.

But just because we went to bed early each night didn't necessarily mean we would go to sleep early. And most nights we would lay awake and talk or play in bed.

If our Dad heard us, he would shout up the stairs, "Go to sleep." But just because he told us to go to sleep didn't mean we could.

It wasn't too bad in winter as it turned dark very early. But in the summer months it stayed light well up until ten o'clock and the thin curtains did little to keep out the light.

Some of our friends were allowed to play outside much later in the evening and sometimes we could hear them playing out in the back field.

I could never see any reason why we were sent to bed so early. Probably my Mother just wanted us out of her hair.

Our house had two bedrooms, one in front which was our parents' bedroom and the one in the back that I shared with my sisters.

At the top of the stairs was the bathroom, it had a bath and a sink in it and in a cupboard was the water heater. When the house was built it was not yet the practice to put the toilet inside the house but was attached to the house in its own separate little room, which you had to go outside to enter.

In our bedroom was one double bed and one single bed and a dresser and wardrobe.

My sisters and I took it in turns sleeping in the single bed, while the other two shared the double.

The window in our bedroom was fairly large and opened out. We didn't have any screens on the windows because we had very few bugs.

One evening when we heard some kids playing in the field behind our house, we opened the window to talk with them.

"Can you come out and play?" they asked. "Why don't you climb out the window?" someone suggested.

Sounded like a good idea to us. If we climbed out of the window onto the attached back toilet roof, which was only one story high, we could go out and play for a while and our Mother and Dad would be none the wiser. Laura thought it was a great idea and that I should go first.

The roof of the toilet was just off to one side, the bedroom window looked out over the back garden.

Opening the window as far as it would go and with encouragement from my sisters and our friends down below, I was able to get out onto the window sill, and if I swung over far enough could just reach the toilet roof.

I managed to get on the roof but unfortunately not much thought had been put into how I got down from the roof, it being one story high and well I was not very big.

Try as I might I could not find a way down off that roof to the ground. So close!

Suddenly we heard my Dad shout up the stairs, "What's going on up there?"

"Nothing, just going to sleep," answered Laura, ducking back in leaving the window part way open.

The kids all hurried off. Leaving me alone on the roof. Uh oh.

My Dad wasn't so easily fooled.

Next thing I heard was our bedroom door opening and my Dad asking again what was going on, what was all the noise?

"Nothing," said Laura

"Where's Gillian?"

"I don't know."

I plastered myself against the brick wall of the second story so he couldn't see me if he looked out of the window.

Eh, what was I thinking? That maybe he would just say okay and go back downstairs. That was about as dumb an idea as thinking I could climb out of the window in the first place.

My Dad looked under the bed then went and looked in the front bedroom and the bathroom and then coming back into our room I heard him say, "Okay do you want me to get the strap, or do you want to tell me where she is?"

Oh, the loyalty of sisters when the strap gets involved.

"She's out on the roof."

"SHE'S WHAT!"

"She's out on the roof."

My Dad looked out of the window and saw me sitting there.

I just sort of gave him a half-hearted smile and holding my palms up shrugged my shoulders.

"Get back in here," he said, through

clenched teeth, "now."

"I can't, I don't know how," I replied. Shrugging my shoulders again, trying another sheepish grin.

"Okay. Well don't move, just stay put," he said in a surprisingly gentle voice.

He pulled in from the window only to be replaced by my Mother. Oh, the look on her face. "Gilly," she said. She used to call me Gilly.

"Whatever possessed you to climb out of the window, what were you thinking? Do you know how dangerous that is, why you could have fell off roof and been seriously hurt."

Suddenly my Dad reappeared in the yard below.

"Bette," he said, looking up at her in the window, "just keep quiet, I'll deal with this."

I saw my Mothers head retreat back into the bedroom.

The kids had all started to wander back behind our house and watched the scene with great interest.

I stood up and waved at them and said "Hi," from my perch. Then I heard, "Gillian!" from below, and "You kids clear off!"

Everybody went running, I shut my mouth.

Going into the shed my Dad brought out his ladder, put it up to the side of the house and very slowly helped me down.

I was amazed he was so calm and quiet and didn't shout at me or anything.

Not until I was safely at the bottom of the stepladder, then he let loose.

He didn't bother going to get the strap, he grabbed a hold of my arm, spun me around and spanked my bum till I saw stars and it started stinging, and I started crying, which I must say I had not done in a long time. Oh, I had faked it a few times to get out of trouble but this time it was real.

We got a good lecturing that night.

After the lights went out and our parents had gone back downstairs, I was still choking back a few last sobs, my bum and my pride still stinging.

We weren't always bad. Sometimes we were very good. We didn't have to be told to do the dishes, well most of the time we did them without being told. We would take it in turns, one washing, one drying and one putting away.

Sometimes the person doing the dishwashing did put extra dishwashing soap in the water and make lots of suds, and we would have suds fights, but we always wiped up all the water afterwards.

We made our beds in the morning, although I must admit sometimes, we only pulled up the top cover and we always put our own clothes away even though they weren't always folded and as we grew taller did the ironing, and ran the sweeper once a week.

Now my sister Laura was a bit of a con artist and she would often tell me how well I did a certain job, like washing dishes or making the bed and that I could do it way better than her, and she would say, "Gillian, why don't you show me how good you are at washing dishes, I can never seem to do it as well as you."

With pride I would do the dishes or make up the bed. It never occurred to me that I was being conned.

When Auntie Annie saw us doing our jobs around the house she would say, "To look at you three you'd think butter wouldn't melt in you mouths."

My Mother said we reminded her of the nursery rhyme:

There was a little girl
Who had a little curl
right in the middle of her forehead,
and when she was good,
she was very, very good but when she was
bad, she was horrid.

26

SUMMER HOLIDAYS

Every summer our Dad would take the family on holiday.

These are some of my happiest memories.

We would usually go camping down in Cornwall.

I think Cornwall is the most beautiful part of England.

Cornwall is a county on England's rugged southwestern tip, forming a peninsula which is surrounded by wild moorlands, lots of sandy beaches and picturesque harbor villages.

The end of the peninsular is called Land's End, with towering cliffs and crashing waves below and on a windy day the spray reaches all the way to the top.

Our usual spot was St. Agnus on the northern side of the peninsular.

We would rent a spot in a farmer's field to pitch our tents for a minimal fee and he would provide us with all the amenities.

It was just a short walk into the village where we could buy supplies at the local grocery shop.

St. Agnus, Main St.   *St. Agnus Bay.*

The streets were narrow and only one car at a time could pass through. And the main street led right down to the sandy beach that was surrounded by towering cliffs.

The sea, though always cold, would be clear and sparkling blue and sometimes you could see seals swimming in the depths. Cornwall was also known for its warm, sunny, summer climate.

Our Mother and Dad let us wander at will.

Sometimes we would climb the hilly pastures and at the top you could see the beautiful blue sea below. Or go down to the beach and play in the water.

When the tide went out it would leave tide pools in the craggy rocks that surrounded the cove and we would find all kinds of creature's trapped there by the outgoing tide. Sea anemone's, crabs and little fish.

Once we found a large crab, and we pulled the poor thing out of the water and wrapped it in a towel to take back to the camp to show everybody.

On the way back, as we went through the village we passed by the local café.

The owner was standing outside and he asked us what we had all wrapped up in the towel.

When we showed him our crab, he offered to buy it from us for two shillings and sixpence. We jumped at the chance. We were rich!

We bought ice cream and chocolate bars and ice lollies and whatever else we could think of until every bit of it was gone.

At the camp site there were usually several other campers and our Mother and Dad would start up conversations with them and we would play with their kids.

We had our own tent and our Mother and Dad had one of their own.

We slept in sleeping bags and I always thought that this was the most wonderful place on earth.

We would awake early in the morning to the smell of frying bacon and our Mother would have breakfast and a hot cup of tea for us all.

The morning fog that would rise off the sea would envelop us in a silent, chilly mist and we would very often eat our breakfast with our sleeping bags wrapped around our shoulders.

But soon the sun would burn it all away and another glorious day would be ahead of us.

In the evening we would light a fire with the wood we had either gathered in the hedgerow or bought from the farmer. And we would all sit around and laugh and talk and some of the other campers would join us or our Mother and Dad would go over to their camp. I think my Mother and Dad were very happy there.

I remember on one of our holidays being awakened in the middle of the night to the sound of rain beating on the tent. It sounded wonderful and we snuggled further down in our sleeping bags.

But unfortunately, we had camped at the bottom of the hill and soon water started seeping in under the tent.

Our Dad rushed over and told us to all go get in the car. They were getting wet too.

We all got soaking wet and spent the night huddled up in the car all wet and soggy.

When the sun came out the next morning, we had the daunting task of drying everything out.

We hung our sleeping bags and towels on the car and neighboring tree branches and our Dad tore down the tents and pitched them further up the hill in case it rained again.

It didn't spoil our holiday. It was just another thing to laugh about.

Each year, when we went camping, we would always go to the same place. We would usually arrive late afternoon after a long and exhausting car ride.

You must remember this was before super highways and the roads we travelled would take was through small villages and wind past farmers' fields with their quaint farm houses, and up hills and down valleys.

The only bad thing in the whole trip was that I was a terrible traveler, getting car sick each time we went anywhere in the car. Shortly after leaving home we would have to make several stops along the way for me to throw up.

But it was worth the discomfort because when we got there, we would have one glorious week ahead of us.

When we arrived in St. Agnus, we would go directly to the farmers house, who rented out his fields, to pay our camping fee for the week before setting up our tent.

The farmer had several fields and from year to year we were not sure, until we got there, just which field he was renting out that year.

One year on the way down, heavy rain delayed us, and we were running way behind schedule.

When we finally got to the farmhouse, we found all the lights off and everybody already in bed.

So, my Dad said we would just go pitch our tents in one of the fields and he would go see the farmer in the morning, after we had a good night's sleep.

We left all our gear in the car only taking out the tents and sleeping bags.

After the long drive we were all exhausted and soon all were fast asleep.

The next morning, we woke to sounds outside the tent and assumed it was our Mother preparing breakfast.

Poking our heads out through the tent flap we all started to scream. We were completely surround by a herd of cows nonchalantly chomping at the grass.

"Dad," we screamed again, which promptly brought him scrambling out of his tent.

When he saw the cows, well, he couldn't help but laugh. We didn't think it was quite so funny.

He bundled us back into the car, picked up the tents and sleeping bags and we made our way back to the farmhouse. The farmer also had quite a good laugh.

We were directed to the right field and soon my Mother had breakfast on and now with the cow's safety behind a fence we thought it was funny too.

27

BUTLINS HOLIDAY CAMP

Butlins Holiday Camps were, the go-to destination for the English population of discerning families for a *'once in a life-time'* family holiday.

But unlike the Disney World of today this was a much simpler time and instead of lights and castles and parades down main street, Butlins had knobbly knees contests and sack races.

English holidays were always a game of chance, you either enjoyed a week of sunshine, beaches, outdoor picnics and fun, or you spent the week in your cabin trying to entertain yourself while it poured rain outside. We were lucky we got a great week of sunny weather.

When my Dad announced that he was taking us to Butlins Holiday Camp for our summer holidays we could not have been more excited and couldn't wait to tell all our friends.

Now, none of us had any idea what to expect we just knew everybody wanted to go there so we did too.

In those days there was not the option of just jumping on an airplane to go to exotic places, it was the only option most English holidaymakers had to get away.

But this was, as advertised: *'A place for families and everyone from toddlers to the elderly were catered too.'*

The Butlins Holiday Camp covered about a hundred acres of winding streets, woods, lakes, cabins, a dance hall, swimming pool and a cafeteria.

You left your vehicle outside the gate and you wouldn't see your only means of escape for the whole week.

It was a very controlled *'Fun for the whole family'* atmosphere and their motto was, by God you will enjoy yourself come hell or high water.

The first thing they did when we arrived was assign us a cabin. It was a small affair with two bedrooms, bathroom facility's and well that's about it.

Remember no televisions or telephones.

A young woman was assigned to us and she would be our guide and go-to girl for the whole week.

The guides were called *'Red Coats,'* because they all wore red jackets.

After we settled into our cabin, she took us on a short tour of the points of interest, like the swimming pool, where we could rent bicycles and roller skates, where the entertainment hall was, and the location of the cafeteria, where we were served our meals promptly at designated times.

The cafeteria was a large affair with several rows of long tables and not only was there a specific time to eat but also a specific seat to sit in, so you would sit next to the same people for every meal.

My parents became friends with the couple who sat across from us, and after we had been there a few days my Dad jokingly asked the man if there was *'an escape committee.'*

After the tour we were left to our own devises and able to explore our new surroundings.

That first day went well.

The weather was warm and sunny, and we walked around familiarizing ourselves with all the features that were at our disposal for the whole week. The large swimming pool area was brimming with people. Adults sitting around in deck chairs and lots of kids splashing around in the water. A snack bar offered hot tea and biscuits for the adults and ice cream cones and ice lollies for the kids.

We rented two four-wheel tandem bicycles. Laura and our

147

Mother on one and Dad, Stella and I on the other. It was great fun. although I couldn't reach the peddles, but I did help steer.

Everyone was expected to go to bed early so there were no late-night parties as the emphasis, as always, was fun for the whole family.

Much to our shock the next morning, bright and early we were awakened to the sound of a blaring loud-speaker blasting out music, only to be interrupted by a sickeningly happy voice telling everybody to rise and shine and make ready for a hearty breakfast and a day filled with fun and laughter.

After we all got over the shock of the rude awakening and our hearty breakfast, we planned out our day.

Our first order of the day was to go to the swimming pool, all of us turning blue from the cold water.

But when they had an event each afternoon and evening, everyone was expected to participate. They had sack races and three-legged races. Knobbly knees contests for the men and a race for the women to see who could get across the finish line first while carrying their husbands piggyback.

One evening was set aside for Square dancing. We were all given outfits to wear that were supposed to resemble what an American square dancer might wear.

148

The Rothwell girls did shine in the Beauty contest. Each of us winning first place in our age group.

Stella in the middle.

And the winner is #56 (me)

First place goes to, Laura with an L

Note the angry clown. Everywhere we looked this stupid clown would be laughing his fake laugh. He was enough to give you nightmares. I think he is why I hate clowns to this day!

And of course, every time you turned around someone was taking your photograph (*black and white*) which could be purchased for the surprising low price of £2 each, so the humiliating photos could follow you through the rest of your life!

Yes, Butlins Camp, I omitted Holiday on purpose, was not the holiday to end all holidays that we had expected and it was with great relief when we walked out through the main gate to our awaiting get-away car.

We did have some fun times though and we can laugh about it now.

Oh, and of course we told all our friends who were green with envy that Butlins Holiday Camp was the best holiday ever.

28

POTATO PICKING TIME

The early part of October was potato picking time.

This was a time that all kids looked forward to because, if nothing else, we got a week off school.

You didn't necessarily have to go pick potatoes if you didn't want to, but there was lots of money to be made so most of us did.

They had started the *'potato picking holiday'* during the latter end of the war in order to get the potatoes harvested in good time before the first frost arrived. Since most men were off fighting in the war, kids were expected to *"do their bit"* for the war effort,

Farmers produced as much food as possible to keep the nation fed. Little food from abroad got through, due to German submarines sinking many supply convoys, so every crop was precious.

Most men, except for the elderly or disabled, were away fighting in Europe so farmhands were in short supply.

And even though they were exempt from joining up, as farming was of national importance, many farmhands felt it their duty and farm labor was scarce.

As the food shortage was coming to an end, at harvest time kids were still encouraged to help bring in the crops. It was sort of a tradition.

It was, for most of us our first paying job and that hard-earned money felt good in our pockets.

Sometimes women would join the potato picking crew for extra income as many families were still struggling to make ends meet.

Each morning about 8:00 o'clock the farmer would drive around the Streets with his tractor and trailer and pick us up, both boys and girls and a few women. Soon the wagon would be full and then he would head for the fields.

We all carried a packed lunch and a thermos of hot tea and our own potato picking bucket.

It would be misty and cold early morning and we would bundle up in old clothes and our Welly rubber rain boots, shedding clothing all day as the day either warmed up or we worked up a sweat with all that bending and lifting.

Our job was to pick up the potatoes turned up by the tractor.

Each of us had a length of field to work. The farmer would go along turning up the potatoes with his tractor and a wagon would follow on behind. We would fill up our buckets with potatoes and then empty them into the wagon on its way back.

It was hard work, bending down all day picking up those earthy potatoes.

Once in a while you would pick up a rotten one and it would squelch between your fingers and stink to high heaven.

On nice days when the soil was dry it wasn't too bad, but if it had rained the night before the fields would be muddy and the potatoes wet and covered in muck and our hands would be filthy and our Wellies got clogged down with mud.

On rainy days there was no work, the tractor couldn't take a chance on getting stuck.

We worked a field until it was cleared then went on to the next one.

The farmer would pile the potatoes into long mounds which he covered with straw and then earth was piled on the top to form a frost-free storage.

Then, over the weeks that followed, the potatoes were dug up again and put into one hundred weight sacks for sale to the shops and markets as needed.

We would work till about noon then sit on the wagon to eat our lunch before resuming work in the afternoon.

Usually we worked until about 4.30 pm.

Sometimes the boys would get into "*spud*" fights, throwing potatoes at each other or we would start fooling around, but then the farmer came along and shouted at us and threaten to take us home with no pay.

At the end of the day we climbed onto the wagon for the weary ride home.

Tired and hungry we would usually go right to bed after our tea.

At the end of the week we were paid our hard-earned wages. It was about two shillings a day.

Ten shillings for five days work seemed like a fortune to us.

Although the women that worked got paid more money than us kids, but after a long week's work, we felt very rich.

It's not long from October to December, so we would try and hang on to our money so we could buy Christmas presents.

Also, we were allowed to take home as many potatoes as we could carry in our buckets, so this was a great asset to the family if all three of us were picking.

29

CHRISTMAS

Christmas was a most exciting time of year. We all believed in Father Christmas *'Santa Claus'* and could hardly contain ourselves waiting for Christmas Eve to arrive.

Christmas for us was in many ways similar to Christmas celebrations of today. Decorations, a Christmas tree, Christmas dinner and presents.

Whereas today the celebrations are often centered more around the gifts than anything else.

My Auntie Annie would spend all day on the 24th making the Christmas feast.

Rationing was still on everyone's mind and I guess we were a little more frugal back then. Decorations like you see today, twinkling lights and animated characters were unheard of. Instead, we made brightly colored paper chains and looped them across the ceiling in the living room. And we would make bells and stars from cardboard cutouts and covered them in aluminum foil.

Holly branches covered in berries, a common shrub in England, graced our fireplace mantle.

We hung tinsel from our Christmas tree to look like icicles and cotton balls to look like snow.

But each year these decorations got more and more elaborate and I'm sure that today they go all out.

We always had a nativity scene, which my Mother insisted on, so we would not forget the meaning of Christmas.

Christmas traditionally began on Christmas Eve. Shops and businesses all across the country would close at noon.

And since we had no refrigerator everything had to be picked up the day before. Which meant a trip to several different shops because we had no supermarket or one stop shopping yet.

Meat from the butcher shop, vegetables from the green grocers.

Alcohol was purchased from the Off License which was usually located in a section of the local pub.

All shops would be closed on Christmas Day the 25th and Boxing Day the 26th.

In years past Boxing Day was a traditional day off for servants. This was the day when they received a *'Christmas Box'* from the master. And even though a custom from the past, the tradition has retained its name and still considered a holiday today.

We would all get dressed up in our best clothes for the Christmas dinner which was served on Christmas Eve.

It was the usual Turkey with stuffing, roasted potatoes, brussels sprout, Yorkshire pudding and gravy.

We always had a Christmas cake and decorated it with tiny figures of Father Christmas, reindeer and tiny Christmas trees.

Auntie Annie would wrap sixpences in cheese cloth and mix them in with the batter and we would all hope to get a piece of cake with a sixpence in it.

A brightly colored Christmas Cracker would sit beside each place setting and after dinner we popped it open with the one sitting next to us for the prize inside, maybe a whistle or a plastic ring.

Then desserts, Christmas pudding, mince pie, trifle, figs, marzipan and nuts.

At bedtime a plate was laid out for Father Christmas, a biscuit and glass of sherry placed by the Christmas tree. A carrot for Rudolph.

Stockings were hung on our bedpost ready to be filled with gifts. Only if we had been good, of course! The stockings would contain a few small items.

When we went downstairs on Christmas morning our gifts were in three piles under the tree. The gifts under the tree, which were from Father Christmas, were never wrapped.

In the early years, an orange and chocolate bar, maybe a pair of gloves. But then as times got better, puzzle books, small toys, crayons and as always, a box of chocolates.

And later a doll and a piece of material that my Mother would make doll dresses for us a few days later, or new roller skates.

One year I got a teddy bear with a music box inside. I could wind it up in bed and it would play me to sleep. It didn't play for very long so I would keep rewinding it, until it got on Laura's nerves and then she would make me stop.

After the Christmas morning presents had been played with, we had breakfast, then we all loaded into the car to go visit Grandma Rothwell and our Aunts and Uncles in Wigan for a glass of sherry or a cup of tea with chocolate biscuits. Then back home again to play with our toys.

Out in the Streets kids were out in full force riding their new bikes or trying out their new pair of roller skates.

Christmas day was a time for leftovers from the Christmas dinner the night before. And then the serving of the scrumptious Christmas cake.

After the washing up, we all gathered around the radio and then later the TV for the Queen's Christmas Day broadcast, when she would wish us all a very Happy Christmas and a prosperous New Year.

Boxing Day was a day of rest, more leftovers and just doing whatever you wanted.

Everything we did concerning family was always centered around the Rothwell's. We knew or saw very little of my Mother's family, although at the time we never thought to question this.

30

GRANNY JACKSON

My Mother was born to Thomas and Eliza Jane Jackson and named Grace Elizabeth, but was more commonly called Bette for short, and she was the youngest of eleven surviving siblings, the next to the oldest having died shortly after birth.

She was born and raised in the tiny village of Hovingham, in the county of Yorkshire on the eastern coast of England.

Hovingham was about sixty miles east of the coal mining town of Wigan, but it just might as well have been a world away.

The village, a quiet sleepy place, was surrounded by lush green meadows that were broken down into a patchwork of tiny fields, each marked off by low stone walls.

A dirt road connected the village with its neighbors and meandered lazily over the rolling hills; it was used by both man and sheep.

The countryside was lush and green, with ridges of woods leading down to broad valleys where farms nestled in rich fields.

And even though there were coal mines in the county of Yorkshire, they had not yet scarred the landscape or polluted the sky with their great clouds of grime.

Her Mother, my Granny Jackson, had a very privileged upbringing.

Being from a somewhat well to do family she had been sheltered from the everyday

problems of life experienced by the *'common folk.'*

Unfortunately, Eliza Jane had found herself pregnant at a young age and since it was not an option in those days to have a baby out of wedlock, she found herself married to Thomas Jackson who, by the standards of the day, was just a common railway worker. And even though his job paid well, their class distinctions would never be bridged.

Eliza Jane found herself suddenly thrown into the life of the working class which left her bitter and unforgiving.

My Grandfather Thomas, by all accounts, was a good looking, hardworking and cheerful young man, but was prone to spend his evenings in the local pub, probably to get away from the biting tongue of his new wife.

But even though their marriage was rocky from the start they nevertheless managed to produce child after child. Twelve in all.

The first five children, including the one that died shortly after birth, were born one after the other. But then there followed several years of no more children.

Who knows why, but the cycle started again a few years later and they would produce seven more.

There was such an age difference between the first set of children and the last set that they grew up as virtually two individual families.

My Mother was the last child Eliza Jane would have and she grew up having little contact with her much older siblings.

Of the seven youngest children, my Uncle Dick and Uncle Charlie where next in line and their Mother ruled them with an iron fist.

Through intimidation and guilt, she managed to squelch every relationship they had and neither would marry until after her death.

Next came Auntie Molly, Auntie Lucy and Auntie Dilla. These three girls seemed to have been pretty much ignored by their mother and so led more normal lives.

Auntie Molly married first and moved out.

My Auntie Lucy joined the army where she met John Maples and eventually went to America.

Auntie Dilla's husband, Ernie was captured at the beginning of the war and would spend his war years in a German prisoner of war camp.

And then there was Bette, my Mother. The last member of this sprawling, dysfunctional family.

She told me once she remembered her father only slightly, but what she did remember, she thought he was kind and loving, though seldom home.

She said she often wondered what he did to make her Mother so angry all the time.

Then one day he just went off to work and never returned.

It was never really known why or where he went, but it was widely speculated that after all those years of living with a shrew, he just couldn't take it anymore, which in my opinion was a poor excuse for abandoning his family and leaving seven children in the hands of a rather unstable Eliza Jane.

Now, my Mother had a brilliant mind and was thought by her teachers to be a gifted child and Eliza Jane was approached by the headmaster to allow Bette to attend a special school for gifted children.

Convinced that the school was just trying to take her daughter away from her Eliza Jane hung on to her youngest daughter with an unbreakable grip and emphatically denied her the opportunity, condemning her to an education in a one room schoolhouse.

Bette was now trapped in her mother's paranoia and could only dream longingly of the outside world with no idea how to join it, stagnating in the little village of Hovingham for the remainder of her adolescent years.

By the age of eighteen my Mother had had little contact with the world outside of the little village, but her thirst for knowledge knew no bounds, self-educating herself with the many books she found in the family attic and at the local library.

But when her sister Lucy announced she was going on holiday to the Isle-of-Man, Eliza Jane insisted that she take Bette with her.

I can only assume that Eliza Jane thought that by having Bette along it would keep Lucy out of trouble and that Bette would report any of her sister's misdeeds when they returned home.

This was the first time Bette had been away from home.

But Eliza Jane's plan backfired because while on holiday my Mother met and fell in love with George Rothwell.

He captured her heart and would, eventually, change her life.

When they met, George Rothwell had a lot of things going for him, he was handsome, had a good job and though not married, owned his own home.

You would think he would be an ideal choice for a husband.

But he had, according to Eliza Jane, more cons than pro's and she felt he was quite an unacceptable suitor for her youngest daughter.

To name a few: He lived in industrial northern Lancashire County with its numerous coal mines and cotton factories. He was ten years her senior, was of the common working class and lastly, in Eliza Jane's opinion, he was a man, and like all men only wanted her daughter for one thing and one thing only.

So, she was vehemently opposed to the relationship, and did everything in her power to put an end to it.

George was not allowed to come to the house and Bette was to have no communication with him under any circumstances.

After two years of making the train trip from Wigan every weekend and meeting Bette in secret or not getting the chance to see her at all, my Dad finally gave my Mother an ultimatum. Either leave with him now or he would be out of her life forever.

In the bravest decision she ever made she left her domineering mother and ran away with the man she loved.

Her mother, unforgiving to the bitter end shut her daughter out of her life altogether. An action my Mother would never completely get over, given the many years of guilt and intimidation that had been heaped upon her and defined her for the rest of her life.

I saw my Granny Jackson twice in my life.

Once in a while we would make the journey to Yorkshire to visit my Aunts and Uncles, but Granny Jackson always seemed to be in-disposed and unable to be disturbed so we never got to meet her.

I think my Mother had only seen her on a few occasions in the intervening years and Granny Jackson didn't seem to have any interest in seeing her three granddaughters.

But then one day our Mother informed us that Granny Jackson had decided she wanted to meet us.

My Mother seemed pleased with this turn of events but was very wary, not being sure what had brought on this sudden interest in her children.

By the time of the upcoming visit we were filled with dread. We had not heard one good thing said about Granny Jackson, and having never met her before, were not sure what to expect.

My Mother spent a frenzied week making us matching dresses with new white shoes and socks and a white ribon to tie in our hair.

I felt like a Princess

On the way to Granny's house

Granny Jackson was living, at that time with my Auntie Dilla and her husband my Uncle Ernie.

Young Ernie Bennett had been a member of the British army at the outbreak of the war. He had taken a week's furlough to marry my Auntie Dilla.

But while on their honeymoon he had been recalled to take part in the massive military campaign to land British troops on the beaches of Dunkirk on the coast of France.

They were greeted on the beaches by the Germany forces and hundreds of British and allied soldiers lost their lives.

So, it was decided to evacuate the entire force by sea in order to save them from certain annihilation.

From May 26th to June 4th, 1940, as many as 338,000 British and Allied troops were rescued.

The massive operation, involving hundreds of naval and civilian vessels, became known as the *'Miracle of Dunkirk'* as a motley armada of English vessels were hastily assembled to facilitate the evacuation, and naval cruisers and destroyers were joined by hundreds of private fishing boats, yachts, and pleasure craft, anything with a draft shallow enough to approach Dunkirk's wide, sandy beach.

Unfortunately, not all were rescued and 90,000 were captured and sent to German prisoners of war camps all over Germany. My Uncle Ernie was one of those unfortunate men and would spend the remainder of the war as a prisoner.

Uncle Ernie had been liberated by the Americans and came back home a broken man. It would take several years before he would recover from the harsh treatment he had endured while a prisoner of war.

They had two children, my cousin Susan who was a year younger than me and my cousin Andrew who was younger than Stella.

All her life Granny Jackson had been afflicted with every malady she could think of to control those around her and on the day of the visit, as usual, she was feeling under the weather and laid up in bed, but she had given instructions that we could visit her upstairs.

A steep flight of steps rose into the darkness, the door at the top was shut.

We followed my Mother up the stairs and when she got to the top, she knocked and then very timidly opened the door and led us in.

We stood, all in a row, side by side, my Mother, Laura, myself and then Stella.

The vision of that encounter is imprinted on my mind to this very day.

The room was large and dimly lit by a lamp sitting on a bedside table next to the big double bed that did little to brighten the murky interior.

Even though it was the middle of the day the windows were covered by thick dark curtains.

Granny Jackson was sitting up in the middle of the bed, plumped up by lots of pillows. A colorful patchwork quilt was tucked around her, which seemed out of place in the dim interior of the room.

She had a white shawl wrapped around her shoulders, tied at the neck with a bow. Her face was plump and ashen and surrounded by gray curls, a pair of glasses perched on the end of her nose. White hands, blue with protruding veins, lay idly at her sides.

On the far side of the bed was a tray with a half-eaten sandwich and an empty cup of tea.

And even though I knew this was my Granny, I felt a trickle of unease run down my spine.

My Mother said, "Mother, this is Laura, Gillian and Stella."

Silence, you could have heard a pin drop, and Granny Jackson didn't make any effort to fill in the silence.

My Mother seemed to pull down a curtain of denial, like everything was normal and smiled at her mother, as if willing the scene to be just as pleasant as she had pictured it.

Granny Jackson just glared at her. Then turned her eyes on us.

Her eyes were hollow that gave nothing away, not even a hint at her feelings.

She raised her eyebrows and looked us up and down one at a time.

Never once through that whole visit did she speak a word to us.

Her first words to my Mother were, "How am I supposed to see them way over there? Bring them closer."

My Mother shuffled us, reluctantly, closer.

Granny Jackson commented on Laura's black curly hair and my crooked teeth and said "The little one, she's all skin and bones." Not one positive statement was said about the three little girls standing before her.

I glanced at my Mother, waiting for her to tell the old witch to go to hell or for Laura to tell her to bugger off, instead I saw my Mother physically shrinking under the gaze of this woman who was her mother.

And Laura's jaws clenched tight shut. She knew that this was not the time to speak her mind.

I felt Stella reach up and take my hand and when I looked down at her I saw the tears spill out of her eyes and down her cheeks. She did not understand what was happening but sensed that something was very wrong.

I realized in that moment we, my sisters and I, were a web of connected hearts. That I was not one single person but part of them and the burden of it was both overwhelming and strengthening. That somehow loving someone sort of made you responsible for them and them for you.

My Granny Jacksons words did not go in one ear and out the other, but stuck right there inside my head, nor did they roll off me like water off a duck's back but lay like a heavy load on my shoulders. I felt such anger welling up inside me.

An anger that I still feel to this day.

After what seemed like an eternity my Mother turned to us and told us to go on downstairs and play.

No goodbyes, or, pleased to meet you were uttered from either side.

We left the room single file, Stella in front.

Stella headed down the stairs one step at a time, hanging on to the banister rail so she wouldn't fall. Stella was still quite small.

Laura and I delayed on the landing as my Mother closed the door behind us.

We could hear their voices in the room and put our ears to the door so we could hear what was being said.

"Did you think you could just come back here after all this time, just walk in here with your brood of children like nothing ever happened, knowing what you did to me? Did you ever realize how lucky you were, you never appreciated anything I did for you, ungrateful that's what you are, ungrateful," we heard Granny Jackson say.

And all the while I'm thinking, just tell her to bugger off, or harden your heart so she can't touch you, let her words just wash over you like water off a duck's back.

But we all have our own way of dealing with things and my Mother said in reply.

"That was a long time ago Mother, why are you still so angry? Please try and forgive me."

"Forgive you, why should I forgive you? I have suffered all these years because of you. You betrayed me," said Granny Jackson. "I am laid up in this bed because of what you did to me."

But then, finally, my Mother replied, "This was just another of one of your cruel tricks, but this time you have gone too far. I had hoped that we had moved on, that you had forgiven me for leaving, but don't worry, it isn't necessary anymore, I no longer need your forgiveness." Then silence filled the air, an eternity seemed to pass.

Finally, we heard my Mothers footsteps coming towards the door and Granny Jacksons voice, grating, shouting, "Get back here, how dare you speak to me that way. You never had any concern for anyone but yourself."

As the door opened, we hurried off down the stairs so she wouldn't know we had overheard.

When My Mother came back downstairs, she tried to act like everything was fine and told us to go on outside and play with our cousins.

We went outside but didn't play much and not much was said between us.

My Mother talked with her sister Dilla and Uncle Ernie for a while before we set off on the long train trip back home.

This incident was never spoken of again. And we never understood why our Granny Jackson didn't like us, nor was it ever explained to us.

A few years later I was to see Granny Jackson again. This time at her funeral.
Laura and Stella stayed home with our Dad, but I went.
Granny Jacksons coffin was taken from the house, where it had sat for twenty-four hours so people could pay their respects, then carried to the Crematorium, the mourners walking behind.
I knew only a few of the people that attended, although my guess is some of them were my Aunts and Uncles whom I had never met, but I was never introduced and nobody inquired who I was.
The coffin was placed on a raised and decorated platform in the front of the chapel.
Then there was a short service. I didn't see one tear shed in the small group of people that attended.
After the service, they pulled a curtain around the coffin so that it hid it from view, and then slowly it was pulled on rollers through a door where the cremation took place.
Then we just all left the chapel. The whole process took no more than thirty minutes.
My cousin Susan was walking with us back to their house.
Looking back toward the church you could see the smoke curling up from the chimney, and my cousin Susan said, "frying tonight."

I couldn't help it; I started to laugh. My Mother did not reprimand me, instead through her tears she too laughed. Then remembering the solemnity of the occasion, we put our somber faces back in place.

We all went back to Auntie Dilla's house for sandwiches and tea, and then my Mother and I made the long train trip back home.

Later that night, Laura asked me, "Why on earth did you want to go to the funeral?"

I answered, "I just wanted to make sure that she was well and truly dead!"

I made a vow that day that I would forgive my Mother for any injustice heaped on me, whether real or imagined because no matter what she did she could never be as bad as that mean old woman in the room upstairs.

31

CLIMBING THE SOCIAL LADDER

With the war behind us and rationing creeping to an end for the citizens of England, life was slowly returning to normal.

Men were finding work and most women were ensconced back in the kitchen.

But many women, who had tasted the freedom of being part of the workforce didn't want to go back into the kitchen, and so the dynamics of the English family was drastically changed.

With many mothers reluctant to give up their jobs, and therefore a certain amount of independence never experienced by women before, and extra cash for the family, a new generation of *'Latch Key Kids'* emerged.

With all three of us now in school, even though Stella was only five there was no longer any need for Auntie Annie. We were now part of the new generation.

We were considered old enough to fend for ourselves. We could get ourselves off to school in the morning and let ourselves in the house in the afternoon.

Saturdays Laura and I could take care of Stella. and of course, Sunday was still family day as everything was closed.

My Mother, who had been raised in a very strict, gloomy atmosphere by her domineering mother nonetheless had been raised to be a lady of refinement. She always spoke well, never picking up the lilt of northern Lancashire like her husband and three daughters.

For as long as we could remember my Mother spoke very little of her growing up years. But suddenly it seemed a door had opened ever so slightly for her into her past and now gave her only positive things to remember.

She seemed to long for that time when young ladies were sophisticated and well mannered.

But with the war and the devastation visited on the country and survival being the main concern, I imagine all these attributes she expected from her daughters had been the last thing on her mind.

Now it was a time for change.

Her daughters needed lessons in deportment and sophistication, albeit a little late, but now must be paid strict attention to.

She very often quoted, "When I was a little girl……," or "When I was growing up……."

She seemed to have totally forgotten the confinements and bitter days of her young life and the wretched woman we had met in the bedroom upstairs in Yorkshire.

The first thing to change were mealtimes. Instead of the hustle bustle of a family dinner, exchanging stories of the day, now it was no speaking unless spoken to, no elbows on the table, no this, no that.

A fully set table was the order of the day. A glass of water for drinking instead of tea, and only to be drank if your mouth was empty. Silverware by each plate, that you would never use, put there to teach us what utensil went with what particular dish.

Always use your knife and fork to transfer food from the plate to your mouth and then lay them back on the side of the plate, put your hands demurely on your lap while you chew and swallow your food, only then could you pick them up again for the next bite.

The way we spoke came next. *'H'* had to be sounded, no more saying *'ouse*, it had to be *house*, no more saying *our* or *mi* when referring to each other, like, *our* Laura, or, *our* Stella, or *mi* Mother or *mi* Dad. *Cold* instead of *'coud.'* Your instead of *'y'r'* and many more words that the Lancashire people had made their own daily spoken brogue.

When she did not see enough progress, she decided that me and our Laura, sorry, Laura and I, should attend Elocution Lessons or in layman's terms, how to speak the Queens English.

Stella was too young, but my Mother took Laura and I by train every Saturday to

Manchester for lessons.

We learned to sound our 'H' by repeating phrases over and over again. Like, *"How now brown cow."* And say the poem, *'The owl and the pussy cat'* over and over again.

I can still repeat it to this day.

Next was poise and posture. Shoulders back, no slouching, cross your legs when seated.

And do absolutely nothing that would give a glimpse of your knickers. This class was called *'Health and Beauty'* and was designed to teach young ladies' deportment and manners.

We tap danced for coordination, we walked around endlessly with a book on our heads for posture, and got up and down from chairs to learn the correct way to take a seat so we wouldn't show our knickers.

Unfortunately, sending Laura and I to these schools was like putting a pair of puppies in the proverbial china shop and the teacher proclaimed more than once that we were hopeless.

My Auntie Annie told my Mother with a chuckle, "Don't be so daft, it's like trying to make silk purses out of a sow's ears, trying to make them two into young ladies."

Unfortunately, my Mother did not see the humor in this and didn't speak to her for a week.

I think the last straw came on the way home from our final Elocution Lesson.

While sitting in a drafty train carriage on the way home, Laura told the man sitting under the offending open window, "Wil'st tha shut that bloody window; it's 'coud' in 'ere."

I think my Mother resigned herself to the fact that indeed you could not make silk purses out of sow's ears after all and gave up.

Dad didn't seem to care one way or another. In her defense, while having dinner in a nice restaurant one day I was relieved to know what utensil to use with my salad and which was the soup spoon, and she beamed when we laid our knife and fork down after each bite, did not talk with our mouths full and did not speak until spoken to. And when we did speak, the 'H's were clearly sounded.

Next came a parade of associations with people of the middle to upper class.

The first one I remember was an elderly gentleman that my Mother referred to as the Major, who spoke like he had a mouth full of marbles, a handlebar mustache, and was always saying things like, "Jolly good show old chap."

He was accompanied by a very young and very beautiful French lady. She wore an elegant light blue suit that matched the color of her eyes and a stylish blue hat with netting that sat perched at an angle on her head. White gloves and silk stockings and extremely high heels completed the look.

I tried not to stare but I had never seen anyone like her before. She looked so graceful and beautiful.

Unfortunately, my Dad thought she was beautiful too and couldn't take his eyes off her either, and so that friendship soon came to an abrupt end.

Another memorable acquittance was a Mr. Fleishmann.

Mr. Fleishmann and his wife lived in Liverpool. They were a portly, German Jewish couple both with the whitest hair. Mrs. Fleishmann was a very dowdy looking woman and always wore a headscarf. But her husband was impeccably dressed with his full head of white hair combed neatly to one side and an impressive mustache that he kept neatly twirled at the ends.

They had been quite well off in their home country of Germany and had lived very well, but with the rise of Hitler, Mr. Fleishmann had seen the writing on the wall and left for the United Kingdom before the Nazi pogroms and persecution of the Jews could confiscate, not only his life but his wealth too, which he was able to escape with pretty much intact.

Mr. Fleishmann's ultimate desire was to take his family to the United States of America but try as he might never could get the permission to immigrate to the country he had learned to love even if sight unseen.

I liked the Fleishmann's. They were a very kind and thoughtful family and they had the most wonderful accent.

How my Mother and Dad became acquainted with them is anybody's guess.

One day we took the train to Liverpool to visit them. Their house was in walking distance from the railway station.

Liverpool had been a thriving city before the war and a strategic port. This made them second only to London to be the most heavily targeted city by the German bombers.

It wasn't just the docks and city center that had suffered under the bombardment, residential areas also experienced vast devastation.

An astonishing 40% of Liverpool's houses were either destroyed or seriously damaged, leaving 51,000 people homeless.

In many areas, large swathes of housing were wiped out as a result of the long barrage.

Much of the city center was rapidly being rebuilt but many houses and business were left untouched for years.

When we arrived at the Fleishmann's street we were met with an incredible site. It was obvious that before the war this had been a very affluent area. But now only a few houses remained standing.

The street had been lined with trees but now only broken burned out trunks and crooked trees were left, a few branches throwing out token leaves in their struggle to survive.

Very few buildings remained intact.

The whole street had been rows of four-story brownstones and must have been beautiful in their day.

This photo is the closest I can come to how the street would have looked before the bombing.

Two homes side by side shared the same steps leading up to the front door with wrought iron rails.

The impressive front door and intricate carved stonework spoke of wealth and prestige.

The house to the right of him was nothing but rubble. The house directly next to him, with whom he shared the steps, was just a shell.

How on earth his house had remained standing is nothing short of a miracle, and the fact that he still lived in it is a testament to the human spirit. The front steps were clean and white, and door and window frames brightly painted. Even the wrought iron rail was black and shiny.

We were greeted very warmly and without apology for the devastating surroundings by Mrs. Fleishmann and very large, friendly white dog.

The first floor was just below street level with steps leading down to a doorway. The main front door was on the second level.

On entry you were in a small vestibule with a stairway on the right and a narrow hallway leading to two rooms, one directly behind the other.

This was a house of several generations, all living there together.

We gathered in the front room, the desolate street outside visible through the large bay window. Velvet curtains from another era blocking out some of the light. It must have been splendid in its day. The couch and chairs, though grand were now threadbare and many beautiful paintings hung on the walls and an elegant clock graced the marble mantelpiece.

We were introduced to the other members of the family, several of them children of various ages and when they asked us if we wanted to see upstairs, we gladly accepted.

Up the narrow staircase the bedrooms seemed endless. The third and fourth floor had three bedrooms on each level and a small bathroom.

And lastly a small enclosed stairway led up to the attic where several of the children obviously slept as there were several beds and toys littering the floor. It was the length and breadth of the house with a window in the front and one in the back.

It was a most fascinating house.

Every wall was hung with paintings and tapestries with large highly polished furniture throughout.

But looking out of the attic windows brought back the reality of the devastation outside.

Nothing but broken-down buildings everywhere you looked.

Going back downstairs they asked if we wanted to see the chickens.

The back yard must have at one time been surrounded by a high stone wall but only parts of it remained. The parts that were missing had been replaced by chicken wire and for a good reason. The whole back yard was one big chicken coup. There must have ten to fifteen chickens pecking around in the dust, guarded by a strutting colorful cockerel.

When we started down the steps, we were warned that the cockerel was very mean and sure enough at the sight of us he came squawking over flapping his wings, and we all rushed back into the safety of the house.

The kids told us that only their Grandma could go out there safely, which she did each morning to collect eggs or to wring a chicken's neck for supper.

The final acquaintance I remember was Mr. Norman Greenwood. This person would have long reaching effects on my life.

32

MR GREENWOOD

My Mother, an avid reader, was interested in everything imaginable. She always had her nose in a book. She would throw herself into one interest after another fully absorbing it before moving on to the next.

One of her many interests were religions.

We were Christians and went to church regularly, but she wanted to understand, not just Christianity but all religions.

She studied them all, from Buddhism, Hinduism, if it had 'isum at the end of it then she would want to know what it was all about. Atheism, Catholicism, Methodism. Orthodox this and Orthodox that.

Through the war we had attended church only occasionally, although more so after my Dad returned home, but it was more practiced in the home than actually going to church, because unfortunately during the war churches were a dangerous place to be.

Their towering spires an irresistible target for the *German Messerschmitt*, and many churches all across England suffered devastating damage.

But St. Ambrose Church of England, our regular church had weathered the storm and came through the war unscathed.

Sunday mornings were a time for church.

First thing we did was polish our shoes. My Dad was a stickler for clean shoes. He often said you could tell all about a man by whether his shoes were polished or not, and I suppose that had trickled down to include children as well.

We would put on our best clothes and off we would go.

After the service all the devout silence was flung off and we excitedly hurried home for the freedom of whatever the day had to offer.

Again, how or where my parents met Mr. Greenwood was anybody's guess.

Mr. Greenwood was a tall gangly man with horned rimmed glasses whose lenses looked like the bottom of a glass bottle.

He was a pleasant enough man. He brought his family to visit and our Mother told us to take their two sons outside to play. They were probably two and three years younger than me. They also had a sister, but she stayed by her mothers' side. She was probably no more than two years old, and Mrs. Greenwood was also pregnant.

Mr. Greenwood was a Methodist. Not only was he a Methodist but the Headmaster of the Methodist School in Leyland, and according to my Mother he was the teacher to end all teachers.

After this visit we started attending the Methodist Church. Which in my opinion was not much different than that of St. Ambrose,

Leyland Methodist Primary School

Begging's and pleadings fell on deaf ears.

My Dad didn't say one way or another.

The Methodist School was attached to the main Church and was built in the same style.

I soon found out, on that first day, that the main focus of the school was religion and everything else seemed to be unimportant.

So, I found most basic lessons to be a breeze, the religious part, not so good. Because even though we believed in the same things they just believed in them in a different way. Quite confusing actually.

The general subjects, these were things I had learned a year ago, so I found easy, but unfortunately being a *'know-it-all'* did not help to ingratiate me with my new fellow students.

Boys and girls were zealously kept apart by the staff, so we had minimum contact with boys during school hours.

There were two separate playgrounds, one for the girls and one for the boys. The ground was concrete and the stone wall that surrounded each was so tall that Jesus himself would have had a hard time climbing over, let alone a boy with ill intent.

Since I had come from a mixed school and both classrooms and playground where shared, and the fact that many of my childhood friends included boys, I found this practice very odd.

Our teachers couldn't emphasize enough the evil ways of boys.

But even though we were separated from the boys, who, according to our teacher, would more than likely try to do unspeakable things to us, they, unfortunately, gave no thought to the evil things that the girls could do to you.

The leader and the boss of the playground was a girl called Linda Moore and her sidekick was Mavis. I can see their faces to this day.

These two were bullies of the worse kind and I became their favorite target from day one.

Most of the kids in the school had been through the same classes together for a long time and knew each other well, not only from school but in their neighborhoods too.

Here I was an interloper in their midst. Not only was I good at my lessons, I was also a pretty girl which did not sit well at all with Linda Moore and I was picked on unmercifully.

Pushed and shoved, my hair pulled, name calling, it never ended.

I would try and keep a low profile but in the close quarters of the playground; there were no hiding places. No teachers ever came to monitor us, and I knew to tell would make matters worse.

My Mother said I was exaggerating so there was no help there, even though Stella tried to tell her what was happening.

It must have been hard for Stella to see her big sister go through this every day and no doubt she was going through much the same herself.

After several weeks of this constant bullying, everything came to a head one day when Linda Moore decided that I should fight Mavis.

I told them I wasn't going to fight and did everything I could think of to get out of it. Not only was I small for my age, I must admit I was also deathly afraid as I knew no teacher was likely to come to my aide.

On the day of the fight all the girls formed a circle around us and when I tried to escape, I was unceremoniously pushed back in.

Mavis pushed me down a couple of times and they all laughed, and she pulled my hair, then punched me in the stomach. As I bent over, the wind knocked out of me, I saw my little sister Stella in the crowd crying and shouting for them to leave me alone.

I realized that Stella was also captured in that web of connected hearts that made you afraid and responsible for those you loved, and that I was not one single person but had a responsibility to her, and that not only was she my burden but I was also hers.

The feeling that I was letting her down was overwhelming. That loving her made me my sisters' keeper.

Something in me snapped.

Never underestimate a child who has been pushed beyond their limit.

I attacked that girl with every part of my being. Self-preservation? Adrenaline? Call it what you will.

Blindly, I punched her, scratched her, I knocked her down and when she was down, I kicked her, and I kicked her and punched her till I couldn't do it anymore. I was vagally aware of all the whooping and hollering going on around me, but nobody stepped in to stop me.

I am not proud of what I did. In fact, I was and still am haunted by that day, disgusted with myself when I saw Mavis's bruised and scraped face and when I heard her sobbing, I realized what I had done. I think she was as much a victim as I was.

As I walked away, Linda Moore came over to me patting me on the back and it was all I could do not to spit in face.

I went over to Stella and told her she didn't need to worry about me anymore.

Nobody told the teachers what had happened, they said Mavis had been running and fell on the concrete and they believed the story.

The girls left me pretty much alone after that. Linda Moore was still my problem, only because she now wanted me to be her friend.

Mavis was on the outs.

Did it end there? No.

from what the other girls said, many girls were just itching to be his girlfriend.

After school was over Stella would Now, as obsessive as the teachers were in keeping the boys and girls separated in school, their obligation came to a screeching halt at the school doors.

When you walked out of school at the end of the day, you were pretty much on your own. The teacher's responsibility of the evil ways of boys came to an abrupt end at the school doors.

It was everyone for themselves.

The only exposure we had with the boys during school hours was as we passed them in the hallway when we changed classrooms.

Boys and girls alike would use this short encounter to pass messages back and forth or boyfriends and girlfriends might touch hands in passing or promise to see each other after school.

This fraternizing was greatly frowned upon by the staff, but it went on anyway.

Quite normal actually. Probably the only normal thing at that school.

Now the boys had their own Linda Moore to contend with and I am sure many boys were bullied unmercifully as I had been.

He was a tall, burly kid with carrot red hair and believe it or not his name was, Richard Strangways. I kid you not.

Unfortunately, Richard Strangways had his eye on me. He would jostle me in the hallway, pass me notes, reach over and pull my hair. You know the usual way a young boy shows his affection for a young girl. Nothing like a little pushing and shoving to let a girl know you fancy her, right? He did not take it well that I did not respond to his advances; he was used to getting his own way. And stand just inside the front door and wait for me, so we could walk home together.

While sharing this memory with Stella her memory was a little sparser than mine. After all she was only six. But she did remember always being afraid, she remembers the name calling and being pushed around. She said her biggest fear was that for some reason I would not show up after school to collect her.

Since Stella and I were the only two kids from Farington, when we went out of the front door, we were the only two headed to the right. All the other kids went left into Leyland because that is where they all lived.

At first Richard Strangways would just hang around outside the school waiting for me to come out and taunt us a bit and generally show off to his mates. I thought if I just ignored him, he would eventually give up and leave me alone.

But I suppose he felt he must prove to his mates he was still top dog and eventually he and a few of them started following us home. Maybe just reaching in and pulling my hair or give me a little shove.

Worrying everyday about the inevitable encounter, I began to think of different ways to avoid him.

Sometimes we would hold back leaving school until he gave up and went on his way. Or maybe try and leave before he did and run until we were out of sight. I faked a few stomach aches so I could leave school early, telling my teacher that I had to collect my little sister and they accepted this.

Once in a while I would wait until maybe a couple of ladies were coming from shopping and were heading our way, and I would go by then jump in step behind them. The boys would leave us alone when adults were near.

I prayed daily for rain, even though Stella and I would get wet on the walk home, it was worth it. I didn't seem important enough or worth getting soaking wet for, or maybe the rain cooled his ardor because Richard Strangways never followed us in the rain.

Now the reader must remember this was a different era. It was 1954 in a country just emerging from a horrific war. Several of our teachers had not gone through the education to even be a teacher but the need had been so great that any unqualified person was put into the position of teacher.

And where were our parents you might ask? My Mother and Dad were busy trying to make a living, plus we had been raised to be independent, self-sufficient. For too long we had taken care of ourselves. Always flying by the seat of our pants. I knew that our survival was entirely up to me.

Plus, the events of this chapter took place over a period of several months, in fact that whole school year. But as you can probably tell, it nonetheless left an indelible memory etched in my head.

As Richard Strangways and his mates became more brazen, more measures had to be applied to avoid them.

The road to Farington was a quiet road but it did have several houses along the way. So, if the boys got too close, we would go up to a door and knock. This, most times, would send them back the way they had come.

If somebody answered the door, I would ask the homeowner if such and such a body could come out to play and when they said she didn't live here, I would apologize and we would go on our way.

If the boys were more persistent then I would tell the person who came to the door that those boys were following us, and we were afraid and more often than not the homeowner would chase them off.

But one time they got pretty close.

Now these boys didn't know we had a 'backs' *(alley)* in our Streets, that was a short cut to our house.

I knew I could outrun them if I was on my own, but not with Stella. So, I gave her the house key and told her to run home as fast as she could through the 'backs' and I would go the long way and we should reach the house at the same time.

She was afraid and reluctant at first, but then she took off running as fast as her little legs would carry her, clutching that key in her hand for all she was worth.

The plan worked. I easily outran the boys and when I came around the corner Stella was waiting for me with the front door open. But this ploy could only work once.

If we were ever caught between houses, I knew we would be in trouble.

We would pace ourselves, running in the open spots, walking to catch our breath as we passed a house, just in case.

But I always knew our luck would run out one day.

The next and final incident happened a few weeks later. Caught between houses, my worst fears were realized.

If I remember rightly there were three of them, Richard Strangways and two of his mates. I suppose to them it was just one big game. They had never followed us this far before.

They caught up with us between houses and Richard Strangways grabbed a hold of my hair pulling me back.

Stella started crying as he pushed me against the wall and laughing tried to put his hand up my skirt.

Fear, outrage and adrenalin my only defense, I swung my school bag with all my force and a lucky shot caught Richard Strangways on the side of his nose and it gushed with blood.

His hands went up to his nose, a shocked look on his face. His mates came running over to him as they saw blood pouring from between his fingers.

Seeing my chance, I kicked him as hard as I could right in his balls and when he doubled over, I grabbed Stella's hand and we ran. I heard him shout to his mates, "Get her," but fortunately we were close enough to home and we made it before they could catch us.

But I knew we were done for. He would never live this one down. His mates had seen him bested by a girl and I knew he would seek revenge.

Now we were really scared.

When you came out of the school's front doors, just to the left, the way all the kids walked home, was the bus stop, and it usually had a queue of people waiting for the bus to Farington. If we could only ride that bus home all our troubles would be over.

My parents always kept shillings in a box on top of the gas meter in our pantry, so they had them on hand when the gas meter showed empty. Never in my life would I have ever dreamed of stealing one of those shillings. The closest I had come was when Laura and I had found one under the meter and tried to buy chocolate bars with it. But desperate times call for desperate measures.

The bus fare from the Leyland bus stop by the school to the Farington bus stop near the bottom of our street was tuppence, but half fare for children. So that meant that Stella and I could ride the bus home every day of the week on one shilling with tuppence left over.

So began my life of crime. I swore Stella to secrecy.

When we went to school the next day with the stolen shilling safety hidden in my pocket, I waited for my encounter with my nemesis.

But Richard Strangways was not in school that day, so we walk home in peace.

But the next day there he was with two black eyes and large swollen nose. I knew this would be the test.

He glared at me in the hallway. The day was interminable.

The story around school was he had got into a fight with a big, older kid and knocked the tar out of him. The other kids' injuries, supposedly were much worse than Richard Strangways, and he went around school all day wearing his busted nose and two black eyes like a medal, but he knew I knew the truth.

As usual Stella was waiting for me just inside the school's front door, we were both scared to death.

As the kids started piling out of the front doors, I grabbed Stella's hand and pulled her into their midst and instead of walking to the right, where, as I had suspected, stood Richard Strangways and his mates, we walked to the left.

When we got level with the bus stop, we moved over and mingled with the waiting passengers.

"Two children's fares to Farington please."

Problem solved.

We rode the bus home every day from school, unless it was raining, then we walked, and nobody was none the wiser. My parents never realized that each week that there was one shilling missing.

Soon Richard Strangways just sort of lost interest in me, and Stella and I spent the last few weeks of school in safety.

33

ARGUMENTATIVE AND ALWAYS TALKING BACK

With the summer school holidays ahead of us Stella and I could relax and put that Methodist School out of our heads for six whole weeks. I would worry about it next term.

Summer progressed along fine. Some nice sunny days and some rainy days.

Friday nights were one of our favorites as our parents would often bring us a treat home from the Market.

Friday evening you would find all three of us sitting on the wall waiting for them to come home to see what they had brought us.

Maybe a small toy, some sweets, or my favorite, a pomegranate which we would use a pin to pluck the juicy seeds out to eat.

During those summer weeks the dynamics of our little sister threesome was making some subtle changes.

Although we were still best friends. Laura was less inclined to go out and 'play', spending more time with friends her own age.

Next year she would be a teenager and her thoughts were leaning more towards boys.

Laura was now in love with the son of the local Cobbler (*shoe repair*) and if I remember rightly, his name was David Cropper.

Our Mother and Dad were doing fine at the Market and all was well.

Getting into the last weeks of August, camping gear started piling up in the hallway in anticipation of our camping holiday to St. Agnes.

Sleeping bags were hung on the line to air out. Tents checked for any holes and cooking utensils washed and repacked in boxes.

We three were deciding what clothes we should take and begging for new swimming suites.

The week before we were due to go, we were shocked to learned that Mr. Greenwood and his family and another family, the Bretherton's, would be joining us on the holiday. We had never met this Mr. Bretherton.

Not only had Stella and I suffered all year at Mr. Greenwoods Methodist school we were now going on holiday with him!

But we knew it did no good to protest so we resolved to have a great holiday anyway.

On the morning of our trip we loaded up the car and headed into Leyland where Mr. Greenwood and Mr. Bretherton lived.

We went to Mr. Greenwoods house first, and he loaded his family into their car, Eric and John and Sarah and new baby Alison who had been born a few months earlier.

Then on to the Bretherton's.

Mr. Bretherton lived in quite an affluent area with a nice big house with a big black four door sedan sitting at the curb.

He had one son, Nigel, a tall lanky, sullen boy about eleven who disgusted us from the start by coming out of the house picking his nose.

Mr. Bretherton was a large mountain of a man with a huge belly and a big fat cigar hanging from his mouth which jumped up and down as he talked. His wife, a mousy looking woman, was half his size.

When they climbed into their car, the son sat in the front seat next to his dad, Mrs. Bretherton sat in the back with some of their luggage.

Then they got in line behind us since my Dad knew the way.

It didn't take long for my travelling problems to kick in and a few miles down the road my Dad had to pull over for me to unload my stomach.

Everybody waited silently in their cars and then we were off again on our way.

It took about half an hour before my problem resurfaced and again the caravan of cars had to pull over.

"Hey Rothwell, what's the problem here?" hollered Mr. Bretherton.

My Dad explained what was happening, and Mr. Bretherton just shook his head.

On my third and hopefully last stop, Mr. Bretherton was noticeably aggravated but thankfully didn't say anything, but when we set off again, he came flying past everyone at a high rate of speed, and a few words were exchanged by my parents.

"Idiot," said my Dad, "'opefully 'e'll get lost." I don't think my Dad cared much for Mr. Bretherton.

But a couple of miles down the road there he was pulled over waiting for us and got back in line again when we passed.

Mr. Bretherton pulled this stunt several more times before we reached our destination and by then everybody was noticeably tense.

After checking in at the farmhouse we went to the field and pitched our tents, and everybody seemed to settle down.

The next day, our Mother said, "Girls, why don't you show the boys around the town?" Great.

So off we trooped, what else were we going to do, the three us, reluctant, the three boys loud and obnoxious?

We stopped into the local gift and toffee shop to say hello to the proprietor, who we knew from several previous visits. But the boy's horseplay soon made us leave and happily when they saw the sea, they took off running, leaving us alone to wonder what kind of holiday this going to be.

If we saw them on the moors, they were usually throwing stones at rabbits and birds and just generally making a nuisance of themselves, with Nigel Bretherton being the biggest and oldest of the three always in the lead, egging the other two boys on.

They pretty much left us alone; they didn't want much to do with *'three sissy girls.'*

We made it through the week without any major problem, except for some of the other campers complaining about the boys running wild and causing problems in the usually peaceful camp. Mr. Bretherton's answer, as always, "Boys will be boys," and I think my parents were wishing that they had come alone.

On the day before we were scheduled to leave it was a glorious day. The sun was shining, and the wind was blowing a nice surf up onto the beach, and the tide pools were full of creatures.

Laura, Stella and I spent most of the day wandering through these pools.

But soon the boys came over splashing us and calling us their usual names, poking at the poor sea anemones with a stick who's only defense was a slight sting when touched but helpless against the stick. We hollered at them a few times to stop but it did little good.

But the unlucky crab was the final straw. Picking it up, Nigel Bretherton pulled off one of its legs leering in our faces while he did so.

Now the tide was steadily coming in and sending a few waves breaking over the rocks.

We were getting very angry and the more we shouted at him the worse he got, calling us sissies as he pulled off another leg.

When I saw the look on Laura's face, I knew she'd had it and trouble would surely follow.

Storming over to that big lummox of a lad, she gave him a mighty punch and a shove and sent him flying back, tumbling over the rocks and into the surf and a wave came crashing in pulling him under, and he came up spluttering.

"Hey, what did ya do that for? He could have drowned," yelled the other two boys and followed that lummox as he ran up the beach to his mother crying.

Our parents were all sitting in a row in their deck chairs higher up the beach and when they saw Nigel running towards them Mrs. Bretherton jumped up in concern, shouting, "Oh my dear, what on earth happened, are you okay luv?"

And Nigel said, between sobs, "She hit me and pushed me down, that one there," pointing at Laura.

"I nearly drowned," he whined.

"Yea, he could have drowned," chorused, Eric and John. "We saw it all."

We just stood there and Laura said, "Did not," and he said "Did too."

Mr. Bretherton said to his wife, "For god's sake quit babying him," and turning to his son, with a hint of scorn said, "And you, stop your wailing, ya big sissy, they're only girls!"

Well things would have probably been okay if Laura had just kept her mouth shut, but since she was '*Argumentative and always talking back*', she walked up to Mr. Bretherton, who was sitting there in his deck chair, with his big, fat, ugly, hairy belly hanging over his swimming trunks and that big fat cigar hanging out of his mouth, and with hands on hips leaned over him and I knew what was coming.

"GIRLS, ONLY GIRLS, WELL THIS GIRL JUST MADE YOUR BIG SISSY SON CRY LIKE A BABY."

Shocked silence, the tension palpable, I thought Mr. Brotherton's cigar was going to fall right out of his mouth.

Mrs. Bretherton gasped, and my Mother just shook her head.

Mr. Bretherton's face turned beet red, I guess he was not used to being talked back to, especially by *'a sissy girl."*

The rest is sort of blurry. My Mother told Mr. Bretherton she didn't know what came over Laura and told Laura to apologize. Laura refused.

Our parents issued lots of apologies on our behalf and a few, "never mind's", and "oh its okay's", were exchanged, then everybody just started picking up their stuff and heading back to camp.

That evening the grownups went to the local pub for a drink, while we all stayed at the tent.

When they were leaving my Dad came over to us and said, "Try and behave yourselves, okay," but then he winked at us and we knew everything was just fine.

It was great having a Dad.

The next morning, we all packed up our gear ready for the long trip home.

Mr. Bretherton left first and thankfully I never saw that man and his family again in my life.

A few words were exchanged with Mr. Greenwood and his wife and then they too set off for home.

Just thankful to be on our own, we just hung around for a while then started our leisurely way back home.

It was a happy trip home; nothing was said about certain incidents on that beach. And except for a couple of stops for me to unload my stomach it was an uneventful ride home.

34

THE ELEVEN +

I said I would explain the ELEVEN + so here goes.

The 'Eleven + was an exam that was taken by students at the age of eleven to determine if they should be given the opportunity for a higher education that was only available in Grammar Schools.

Depending on the student's ability to pass this Eleven + exam was a means to determine whether that pupil was suited to the academic rigors of a Grammar School education.

Prior to 1944, Grammar Schools were only available to those who could afford the entrance fee, but since the elite and wealthy were the only ones with the financial means to send their children to these schools and they only represented 10% of the population, something needed to be done to offset this imbalance.

As the working-class population grew, especially after World War II, the upper class realized that candidates for the upper-class jobs were getting very limited and positions hard to fill.

And since there were probably some very intelligent children in the lower classes that could fill these declining, elite positions made it clear that more children needed to be better educated and a Grammar School education would expose them to this higher learning.

From Grammar Schools came members of parliament, doctors, lawyers, teachers etc.

Up until then children whose parents could not afford these fees were given a very limited education.

These lower-class students were expected to fill the general labor force of factory workers, construction workers, servants, shop clerks etc.

So, in 1944 the government introduced the Butler Education Act that gave every student the opportunity to get a good education.

Grammar and Independent Private Schools chose to examine prospective pupils in their final year of Primary School at the age of eleven with the 11+ exam in order to determine if they were Grammar School material and should be given a place in their school.

For the middle to lower class children, places in these schools were allocated solely upon how well the child did in their 11+ exam.

Unfortunately, no thought was given on how they had done previously. If they had excelled in school prior to this exam, it was not taken into consideration.

Children who successfully passed the exam would gain a place in a Grammar School, whereas those who were unsuccessful went on to a Secondary Modern School.

Now if you attended a Secondary Modern School, everybody, even you, knew that you were already a failure at the tender age of eleven.

Secondary Modern Schools quickly became viewed as places where ungifted children ended up, where they were housed until they were old enough to go to work. They weren't really educated to become anything more.

Now, I wonder what twit in the government made the decision that a child at the age of eleven had reached their potential or the maturity to make the biggest most single determination of his or her future is beyond me.

Not only, at the age of eleven, have you not reached physical maturity, you have certainly not reached the age of your potential learning ability.

If you passed the test, you were among the chosen few, plucked from the working class to be enrolled in an elite school, and hopefully college after that.

Three out of every sixty children taking the test were expected to past. Yes, I said three out of sixty.

Some failed through lack of knowledge, some failed by the overwhelming pressure of the closely monitored exam in an unfamiliar school, but many deciding ahead of time that they would rather go to the Secondary Modern School with all their mates than go to a snooty school that would more than likely look down on them.

I feel that this was the case in my sister Laura's failure of the test. She is a very bright, intelligent person but she and all her girlfriend's, not wanting to be separated, all decided before the test to purposely fail. Don't forget they were only eleven years old.

The test was not only a very daunting and stressful time, but peer pressure more than likely overriding the parents desire for you to pass, being the cause of most failures.

You knew that a lot hung on what happened on that day, but were too immature to understand the implications.

35

BACK TO SCHOOL

With the summer school holidays winding down, and the disastrous summer holiday behind us, it was time for Stella and I to start thinking about the upcoming school year.

Apprehension on what the new year would hold for us filled us with dread.

At least Richard Strangways would no longer be there as he would have already failed or passed his 11+, but either way he would have gone to another school.

I decided to hold off stealing shillings until I knew what the future held.

But to our great relief we were informed that at the start of the next school year we would be returning to the Primary School in Farington.

We also started attending St Ambrose church again.

This was indeed the best news ever and Stella and I started looking forward to renewing old acquaintances.

Now just what had happened to cause this big change of events was a mystery to us, I suppose it could have been the episode on the beach, but I doubt it. I think that it was probably for some other reason but whatever it was I could have cared less.

The first day of school Stella and I walked together with lightness and relief in our step.

When we got there, it was like the previous year had never happened and we just jumped right back into the usual routine.

Walks home after school were a breeze and Stella found a new freedom, very often walking home with her own friends.

After my first week it became apparent to me that, while at the Methodist school I had been at the top of my class, now found myself lagging way behind. Such was the inferior education at the Methodist School.

Now this was the school year that I would be taking my 11+ and whereas many of my fellow students had already decided they were not going to pass so they could stay together or did not want to go to a school with a bunch of snobs my thoughts went along a different track. The 11+ was something I wanted very much to pass.

I devoted every thought to my lessons, trying furiously to catch up.

The school year went along uneventful. But with every passing day my stress level went up as I felt I would never catch up. We didn't have homework or extra schooling although the teachers did dedicate their lessons in preparing us, but no individual tutoring was possible, and my fellow students were way past me on many subjects and I knew I would just have to wing it.

As the time grew closer my apprehension grew, stomach aches a regular part of my life.

The day of the test was in a very controlled classroom in a strange school. Each student sat at a desk with an empty desk between to stop cheating.

The test papers were in front of you and two sharpened pencils. The teacher sat in front with a stopwatch.

At the appointed hour the teacher just said "start',' and there you where, just you and your pencils, the test papers and that ticking stopwatch.

There was a non-verbal reasoning test, math problems and English.

In the reasoning sections, pupils had to go beyond their core subject skills to mentally rearrange shapes, break codes and tackle other tough questions:

Here are a couple of the questions I pulled off the internet, from an 11+ test in 1954.

1) There were 325 pies at the banquet. If one dish holds 30 pies, how many dishes do you need to hold all the pies?

2) A bag holds 47 sweets. How many children can have four sweets each?

3) A bottle of olive oil holds 250ml. A larger bottle holds two-and-a-half times as much. What is its capacity?

4) Which has the greater mass, 3kg of onions or 7lb of feathers?

5) Bridgetown, Barbados is four hours behind GMT. If a plane leaves London at 06:00GMT, write the local time it lands in Bridgetown if the flight takes six hours

I still don't know if I could pass it today.

The worst part was you could not jot things down to try and work it out, you had to do it in your head, with that stopwatch ticking loud in your ears.

Are you kidding me!? I stumbled along trying my best, cursing Mr. Greenwood and his Methodist school and my Mother for sending me there.

When the teacher said pencils down, I felt like crying. Even if you had the last answer, if your pencil was just about to write it down, when the teacher said pencils down, that was it, you were not allowed to finish.

In spite of this a few weeks later my parents received a letter in the mail informing them that I was only a few points off passing and considered borderline and I would be allowed to take the test over in a few weeks. I was going to get a second chance. I was filled with hope.

But I was so nervous the next few weeks.

Each morning I would throw up, I couldn't eat and lay awake at night worrying.

And I failed the test miserably that second time.

I often wonder what I could have done with a Grammar School education. And I wonder what bloody idiot ever thought that the age of eleven was a good time to decide a child's future.

Disappointment is one of the heaviest burdens you will every bear.

36

OUR ENIGMATIC MOTHER

Have you ever posed the question to your kids, when they complained about something that to you seemed quite trivial, "Do you know how lucky you are?" I must confess I have said it, and it usually fell on deaf ears.

Well this was my Mothers favorite phrase.

My Mother was an enigma, both sides of the same coin.

As I said earlier my Dad was the largest influence in our young lives, and although he was not an affectionate man, he was certainly kind and attentive.

He taught us most everything we needed to know. He did all the nurturing, and most of the punishing, which on looking back was well deserved. Our Mother didn't seem to take much interest in us, always distant. She was more like a bystander in our early lives.

But as we grew older, and more independent, my Dad's role in our upbringing began to wane. I think he was at a bit of a loss when it came to female adolescence, especially three headstrong lasses.

As the family dynamics slowly began to change, more and more our Mother was the one meting out the discipline, and eventually the inevitable question would be asked, "Do you know how lucky you are?"

Now this was always a trick question. A 'no win situation' if you will.

If there was silence, she would say, "Well do you?"

"Yes." Whoops, wrong answer.

"Well, evidently you don't, because if you did................!"

Okay, "no." Wrong again.

With a voice rising steadily in pitch, "Well you should. Ungrateful, that's what you are. You never appreciate anything I do for you. Do you know the sacrifices I have made for you three? Ungrateful that's what all of you are. You never have any concern for anyone but yourselves," the pitch now going beyond reason. The original crime forgotten in the tirade.

Eh, these words were beginning to sound vaguely familiar. Didn't we hear them someplace before, like upstairs in that dark bedroom in Yorkshire?

The angry stubborn look on Laura's face.

'Please don't talk back,' going through my head, silently standing my ground, dead pan face, letting it go in one ear and out the other, waiting for her to wear herself out and walk away so we could go on with our 'lucky lives'.

And Stella with her lower lip quivering, and big tears forming in the corners of her eyes. Finally, after a few familiar remarks like, "I used to have to walk miles to school in cold weather." And other terrible things she had endured that we, the ungrateful, had heard many times before until it all became a blur.

And Laura, who couldn't keep her mouth shut any longer, "We have to walk to school in cold weather."

Me, aghast waiting for the explosion. But mostly by this point she had enough and just walked away, wearing her martyrdom like a medal pinned on her chest. And, after she turned and left us standing there, her shoulders sagging in her unknown pain, Laura's face would suddenly unfold, and Stella's crocodile tears would mysteriously disappear. Unfortunately, we had heard it all before and it no longer carried any weight.

Although I often feel Laura was frustrated that her opinion held no weight and I am sure Stella would have given anything for hug. But I feel the 'letting it all roll off me like water off a duck's back' approach made my emotional life a lot simpler.

Then in the evening she would sit in her easy chair reading a book, like nothing had occurred, unapproachable, the scene earlier in the day forgotten.

My Dad sitting across from her with his newspaper, softly whistling to himself, blocking out the friction in the family.

The talk was small and sensible, the words they spoke seemed detached from all emotions.

My Dad had always been a quiet, even tempered man and now as he got older, he became more and more detached and only seemed at ease when he was left alone. If there was a problem, well he no longer really wanted to know.

When bedtime came, he would say, "Okay you three, off to bed." There were no hugs, no kisses, no coming up to tuck us in.

In retrospect I realize now that my Mother's erratic demeaner was most likely because of her dysfunctional upbringing and living through the trauma of the war or maybe her disappointment at not having sons, who knows for sure, but my Mother seemed incapable of showing any affection towards her three daughters.

But at this point in our lives we had no real idea of her early trauma and put this together with the undemonstrative nature of the British people in general; in our house affection was hard to come by.

I suppose it never occurred to our parents to explain to us the reason for our Mothers bouts of hysteria that would be followed by a debilitating headache, crying uncontrollably and eventually taking to her bed.

We were only onlookers not participators in our parent's personal lives.

So, it was hard for us to understand her lack of affection for us, or any pain she might herself be going through.

But on the other side of the coin, she did what she could for our well-being, she would stay up late into the night on her treadle sewing machine making us clothes so we were always dressed nice. She made sure we bathed, brushed our hair and cleaned our teeth. We were well fed, kept warm in the winter, and allowed all the freedom we wanted but she seemed incapable of any closeness. The only thing lacking in our lives was a Mother's love and affection.

I believe she loved us but was just incapable of showing it. I must admit though, looking back we were probably a handful and a little hard to love. None of us had any of those cute little girl traits, well maybe Stella did.

But in contrast she was very loving and affectionate towards our Dad. She dedicated her life to him. Everything she did revolved around him. It was more like an obsession than anything else.

But it seemed the more attention she gave him the more he seemed to withdraw. If she took hold of his hand, he would gently release it. If she tried to hug him, he would move away.

She would try and satisfy his every need. Unfortunately, he didn't have many of them. He was a quiet man, said little and demanded less.

To say that my Dad tolerated my Mother's affections is too harsh, it was more like he deflected them. She always seemed starved for his attention. It's a pity he didn't want or appreciate these attentions. It would have been a lot easier on all of us.

We have spent a lifetime, my sisters and I trying to understand our Mother and just where we fitted in. It always seemed that she was just out of our reach, like there was a wall that sealed her off. Our Mother reminded us on several occasions that George was first her husband, then he was our Dad. She built a wall that surrounded him. Unfortunately for us he didn't seem to notice.

When my Dad passed away in 1998, none of us where there for his funeral.

My absence was at her request and not my choice, she had wrenched a promise from me years before. She said that when he died the grief would be hers and she did not want to share it with anyone, not even his daughters. She told me that her years of dedication and sacrifice to him had earned her that right.

I stayed home. I kept my promise.

Stella was also living in America when he passed. She is suffering from multiple sclerosis and could not make the journey. And Laura, wishing to get away for a while, had gone on holiday to India and could not get back in time.

I think the relationship with our Mother was hardest on Laura because she lived near to them for the better part of her life. But only in the few months before his death my Mother had allowed her to get close to him.

But in his dying moments she too had been excluded, for at the end my Mother pulled him back into her world and would not give up one tiny portion of him to share with any of us.

Laura, who had stuck by her through those final days before his death, was ultimately shut out at the end.

I know you will think we exaggerate and are unnecessarily harsh. But even after his funeral, without any of us in attendance, she received his ashes and then refused to tell us where she had scattered them.

She took his final resting place with her to her grave.

But now that she too is gone, I realize what I have lost in her living voice. Her quick-witted intelligence, all her knowledge accumulated over the years of her life. All the things she had lived through, the relationship she had had with our Dad. All the things she might have kept from us, are all now lost forever.

But we are foolish as teenagers, we say and do the wrong things and look for someone to blame for our own shortcomings. What I am now was formed by whatever happened to me growing up.

I owe who I am today to my parents, especially my Mother.

37

ORRELL

With my dreams of a Grammar School education in tatters, it was time to start thinking about the new school year at the Secondary Modern School.

Laura said the lessons were easy, also I would be at the same school as her, so that wasn't so bad and most of my friends had also failed the 11+ so they would be there too.

Although, this was going to be a far bigger school because all the students from the surrounding area who had failed would also be going to the same Secondary Modern School, it was huge.

While all my attentions had been on school lots of other things were taking place at home that would again change my life.

My Mother and Dad were doing very well with the shoe selling business and financially we were in a very enviable position.

About that time my Dad became reacquainted with an old school mate named Bill Brown and they decided to go into business together making shoes. So, my Dad invested all his hard-earned money and together they started a small shoe factory located in Wigan, my Dad's hometown.

But the biggest surprise of all, my Dad was building us a new house.

This news came as quite a shock to not only us but to our Mother also. Whether she wanted to move to Wigan I have no idea. But she was very excited, as we were, about having a new house.

He had bought a lot in a new development on the outskirts of Wigan in the small village of Orrell.

This would not only put my Dad close to his shoe factory but also closer to his family.

Now every Sunday we made the trip to Orrell to see the progress of the new house. It was at the bottom of a cul-de-sac, #39 Hayes Road.

It was all very exciting.

I wasn't too concerned about changing schools because I would have changed schools anyway, but I felt sorry to be leaving all my childhood friends behind.

The new house was made of red brick and had a beautiful bay window in front. It had three bedrooms upstairs, a bathroom and separate room for the inside toilet. This was a great improvement over the Glouster Avenue house where you had to go outside if you felt the need. No more chamber pot under the bed. It all felt very posh.

The downstairs had a nice, spacious kitchen, a front sitting room and in the back a living room that overlook a large back garden. There was a fireplace in both rooms. We still did not have central heating.

The back garden bordered on to a farmer's field with a park on the other side.

On my last visit to England, a few years ago, my Mother, Laura and her husband Aiden and I drove by to look at the house for old times' sake. That farmers field is now a six-lane motorway separating the house from the park, and the road we walked along to go to school is now a motorway bridge.

We knew my Dad would thoroughly enjoy his back garden and have it full of flowers in no time.

And, my Dad pointed out, "Best of all it has a garage."

The house was completed before the new school year started and the prospect of another school was a bit daunting. Not only was I losing all my friends, I had to make new ones.

My new school was St. James Secondary Modern and was about half a mile from our house. Now when they say Secondary Modern, the emphasis being on Secondary, it meant just what it implied. Secondary Modern Schools were less disposed than Grammar schools to promoting academic achievement.

So, once a student entered a Secondary Modern school, irrespective of the student's level of intelligence, the student faced enormous challenges attempting to further their education or making progress for their future. The fact that they were in a Secondary School in the first place meant they had already failed.

A University education was now beyond my reach. And it was generally decided that a Secondary Modern Schools' education condemned a student to a lifetime of social exclusion and self-doubt.

It was almost as if the teachers had given up on you already. If we learned anything, great. If we didn't, who cares. We were not going to need it anyway.

The Secondary Modern School was a far cry from my earlier years in a Primary School where at least they were trying to teach you something and had not yet given up on you.

I was very disappointed.

I knew right from the start that this was not for me. There just had to be more!

I had an active mind and I truly wanted to get an education, to do something with my life, anything!

Many of our classes separated boys from girls so that each sex could learn their own special jobs in life.

Boys were taught how to build and repair things and practiced on school properties such as chairs, desks and fences, as part of their practical training. How convenient for the school, free labor.

The girls. We were taught home management, to prepare us for the lives we were likely to encounter in the future, like cooking and ironing. IRONING! YOU WANT TO TEACH ME HOW TO IRON?

Yes, in home economics we were taught how to iron, especially men's shirts! And the correct way to crimp the pastry on a pie.

I went from trying to solve equations to which part of a man's shirt I should iron first for the best results.

Oh, we still had history, geography, reading, writing, arithmetic and physical education, classes, but they were rudimentary at best.

In the final years of my academic education, I never got any further than multiplication and long division! Nouns, pronouns, grammar, why did I need it? For the future? I wasn't going that way anyway. It's not like I was ever going to write a book or anything!

Physical Education for the boys included cricket, football, known in America as soccer, running, high-jump and long-jump.

The girls played rounders, which is very much like American softball, also running, high-jump, long-jump and field hockey.

All sports were played during school hours, there were no extracurricular activities, no other schools to compete against.

I was quite good at sports. I had always been a bit of a tom-boy, but since we didn't compete against other schools, I never really knew if I was good or not.

Even though academics at the school was soft, punishment could be brutal.

There were lots of rules in that school and punishment for severe crimes harsh and only meted out by the headmaster, Mr. Clark.

The decision to send someone to the headmaster's office was purely at the discretion of the teacher in whose class the infraction had occurred.

If you committed a minor infraction, like being late for class, talking during the lesson or chewing gum then, the teacher in whose class it had taken place could set their own punishment, like writing on the blackboard one hundred times the said crime you had committed, standing in a corner or a rap across the knuckles with a ruler. But for infractions such as, fighting, talking back to a teacher, smoking or copying other students work or worst of all cheating, then it was off to the headmaster's office.

Some teachers were more lenient than others, like Mrs. Tinsley who would often give you a warning or a second chance. But some teachers, like Mr. Humphry the history teacher, were notorious for sending students to the headmaster's office at every opportunity, especially the boys. He was a miserable, mean man.

Punishment at the hands of Mr. Clark could be pretty brutal at times.

Punishment was by the cane, which was swung at your open hand at a high rate of speed.

You had to hold your hand out horizontally in front of you, and if you flinched or moved your hand, it was repeated twice. Most caned students did not tell their parents when they got the cane because there was a good chance that another punishment was given out when they got home.

When I first started at St. James's, of course I didn't know anybody, but I soon learned who the *in* crowd was and I definitely wanted to get into the 'in' crowd, I didn't want a replay of Mr. Greenwoods Methodist School.

Because I was new to the area, the boys were quite interested in the new girl, but I was older now and knew more how to handle them.

But I knew my first challenge had to be the girls.

After a few weeks I got my chance to really prove myself, but it had consequences that I didn't count on.

It was just after our mid-morning break; Mrs. Tinsley was going to be teaching our next class. Reading and writing, which were my favorites. She was a little late coming in and there was much chatter and fooling around, especially by the boys.

One of the boys, on a dare, jumped on and off his desk to lots of hooting and hollering.

It looked like a good idea at the time.

Of course, my timing was off and just as I was jumping down Mrs. Tinsley walk in.

I knew any other infraction I could have got away with but this. I did understand that my goose was well and truly cooked. I had committed an infraction that could not be overlooked, even by Mrs. Tinsley.

I had never been to the headmaster's office before although I had seen the punishment he meted out and I was scared to death.

When you got sent to Mr. Clarks office you didn't actually go into his office, instead you stood outside in the hallway, along with anybody else who had been sent there and you waited. It was mostly boys who got the cane but once in a while, like today, there was a girl.

When I got there, there were already two boys ahead of me and shortly after another boy joined us.

Nobody said anything because that would have been another infraction.

Now, canings were done either during the morning break, the lunch break, the afternoon break or right after school. The reasoning being that other students witnessing the punishment, presumably, would be deterred from doing likewise and so Mr. Clark encouraged everyone's presence when meting out his punishments, always doing it when he knew the hallway would be crowded.

There were many days when nobody was there for punishment but sometimes, like today there were a few. The fact that a girl was getting caned created a lot of interest.

The students didn't congregate to laugh or jeer at the hapless criminals but rather to offer support and kids who didn't cry were held in high regard. Those who did cry weren't made fun of but rather just ignored or patted on the back.

By the time lunch break came I was a nervous wreck and prayed I could stand up to the caning and ruing the fact that I had been such a showoff.

Now, when I first started at St. James's Secondary Modern School, I was aware of a very handsome boy named Johnny Atherton. Johnny was extremely popular with both boys and especially the girls, even ones older than him.

He was tall, much taller than most of the other boy's, even as big as the teachers, the best at sports and what's more, extremely good looking and all the girls would swoon when he walked past. I, like all the other girls, was thoroughly love struck.

But I knew I didn't stand a chance, so I didn't really bother.

Now on this, the worst day of my life, I noticed him standing with his mates in the crowd and my heart sank because I knew I was going to make a fool of myself and cry in front of the coolest kid in school.

Everything went quiet when Mr. Clark, cane in hand walked out of his office. The strange thing was he never spoke to us. I was expecting a long lecture on the evils of disrespect and misbehaving.

He just got right down to the business at hand.

We were all required to hold out our right hand and wait. Once you had been caned, you had to wait until everybody else got their punishment.

He didn't care if you hollered out, or if you cried or if you bent over and held onto your hand to lessen the sting, just as long as you stayed put.

When my turn came, I thought I would be sick. With my hand held out I waited for the pain.

Now, it's a natural reflex to try and protect yourself and at the last second, I pulled my hand away.

An audible gasp could be heard from the crowd and I realized, too late, that I had done the unthinkable. Moving your hand to avoid the cane was punishable by an extra swipe.

I put my hand back up, then feeling such a rage and hatred growing in my stomach, and I knew instantly that I could get through this. So, I clinched my other hand into a tight ball and looked that Mr. Clark right in the eyes. Thwack! The cane came down, and I did not flinch but kept staring at him and then Thwack! It came down again.

Surprisingly it didn't hurt as much the second time, probably because my hand was already numb. I saw the cane go up again and I thought I was getting another for my insolence, but it came down on the last boy in the row and just like that it was all over.

Then Mr. Clark just turned around and went back into his office closing the door behind him. He still had not spoken the first word to us. After he was gone, the crowd surrounded us. Nobody had cried so it was a good day. My friends gathered around me and I knew I was finally '*in*' with the right crowd.

This day had definitely been worth it, and it was to get even better.

Johnny Atherton separated himself from his mates and came over to me. "Good going," he said and sort of ruffled my hair. He was a lot taller than me.

Then he just walked away. Yes, indeed this was a good day after all.

After lunch everyone went back to their class. Johnny was in the same class as me but didn't look my way or talk to me anymore that day, but that was okay I'd had my moment.

By halfway through the afternoon my hand was so swollen I couldn't hold a pencil so Mrs.

Tinsley sent me to see the nurse. I think she felt sorry she was the one who had sent me to the headmaster's office, and she looked at me with sympathy, so I silently forgave her.

The nurse took one look at my hand and told me to go home and soak it in Epson Salts.

She grumbled a lot while she was looking at my swollen hand, commenting on how appalling it was the unnecessary cruelty inflicted on helpless children. *(I have since learned that Mr. Clark was dismissed as headmaster shortly after I had left school for good for unnecessary cruelty inflicted on helpless students!)*

It would take several years before this form of punishment was banned in English schools.

When I got home, I tried to keep my hand out of sight but at teatime my Mother noticed it and asked what had I done. I told her I had got caned. And she said, "Well, I hope you learned a valuable lesson."

The next morning, I was off to school in spite of the injury to my hand, and yes, I had learned a very valuable lesson; I never got the cane again.

I met up with some of my mates on the way and by the time we got to school there was four or five of us, we were all laughing and talking about nothing in particular, but there was some oohing and hawing about my injured hand. I was a hero.

When we got close to the school gates, we noticed there was a gang of boys hanging around, some sitting on the wall, some punching each other and some just generally messing about. Johnny Atherton was there in the middle of them and when he saw us, he broke away and came over to me.

"'ow's 'yu're 'and? Did 'yu're Dad get mad at you?"

"My hands okay," I said and showed him.

And then he said, "tha knows I was real proud of ya yesterday." Then with his hands deep in his pocket he just sort of looked at the ground and kicked an imaginary stone, then said, "Do ya think

I could walk ya 'ome after school?"

Whew, I was in seventh heaven, the girls looked at me enviously.

Johnny Atherton walked me home after school that day and I was his girlfriend from that day forward until I left school three years later. Some things are just worth it.

Johnny lived in the village of Billinge which was a couple of miles from school in the opposite direction than me so when he walked me home, which was about two or three days a week, he would take the bus home.

Sometimes he came to my house in the evening, then he would ride the bus both ways.

My parents didn't seem to mind I had a boyfriend even though I was only twelve at the time. But things were a lot different in England then.

Johnny and I became the best of friends, always hanging out together. Easy talk between us.

When he came over, he didn't come to the house, instead he would let out a loud whistle outside and I would go out and meet him. If I didn't hear his whistle my Dad would shout,

"Gillian, he's here."

Most times when he came over, we would go to the park and meet up with friends.

Once we walked into Pemberton, another little suburb of Wigan, and went to the pictures. The Wizard of Oz was showing, and it was the first time we had seen special effects and a movie in color. We were mesmerized.

On Valentine's Day, he actually came to the house; he showed up at the front door carrying a big heart shaped box of chocolates.

My Mother answered the door, then called to me, letting me know that Johnny was here. I was surprised because this was the first time he had actually come to the door.

Then my Mother looked at the box of chocolates in his hand and asked him why were there teeth marks on the lid. Johnny said he had to climb down from his bedroom window with the box between his teeth because he didn't want his dad to know he had bought a girl chocolate because his dad would think he was a sissy.

Nobody had phones in those days so if for any reason he couldn't make it, I had no way of knowing and was always very disappointed if he didn't show up.

Likewise, if I had to go somewhere when he was supposed to come over, he made the bus ride for nothing.

But while school was in it was nice because I saw him every day through the week.

In a Secondary Modern School, at the age of fifteen you had finished your 'Education Required by Law' and if your birthday fell before the end of the school year, well, you just didn't go back anymore.

Since my birthday was in March my schooling came to an abrupt end in 1959.

No certificate saying you had finished your education was given. No ceremony to mark the day or congratulations was given, after all it was only a Secondary School, you just didn't go back anymore.

Unfortunately, Johnny Atherton didn't turn fifteen until the middle of September, consequently he still had another year to go.

Since I had left school and he didn't, our courtship soon fell apart, mainly because of the lack of the ability to communicate and secondly, I was a working girl now and frankly didn't want to go out with a schoolboy.

When I first left school, I experienced, like most kids, an elated feeling that I was done with school. But I had a keen mind and soon regretted not being able to continue my education.

Now I was a part of the general work force. At fifteen my future was already decided. My prospects were grim.

My first job was at our local Green Grocery Shop just around the corner from our house.

These little Green Grocers Shops, in those days, were just about on every street corner and they were greatly depended on by the locals.

They sold everything imaginable. From canned goods to fresh fruit and vegetables, sweets and tobacco. And you could always find the local newspaper, and news from the shopkeeper about what was what in the neighborhood.

Most of them were run by one family which bore their name over the stores front window and who, more often than not lived on the premises with the shop being in front and the living quarters behind and upstairs.

Mr. Gaskell had been in business for a long time and was a nice man, but I soon got bored and dissatisfied and didn't stay there for very long.

Then I just jumped from one menial job to another, restlessness and dissatisfaction dogging me.

38

LITTLE IRENE

At one of my short-lived jobs, stuffing advertisements into envelopes, I met a girl named Irene Ashton and we became inseparable best friends. In fact, she visited me in America many years later.

She was a very unique girl. She had the longest natural blonde hair, a beautiful face, was petite everywhere except she had the largest bosom I had ever seen, she looked like a playboy centerfold in miniature. Irene was only 4'8" tall.

Being of small stature myself, just 5', she was the first person my age that I was taller than.

Her mother and father, though very heavy, were both extremely short people too. Her dad owned a local neighborhood pub and she and I hit it off right away.

I often invited her to my house, and she came over every chance she got, often eating meals with us and once in a while staying overnight.

She never invited me to her house; she said she was too ashamed. She lived in a very poor part of Wigan.

On her sixteenth birthday, about a month after I had turned sixteen, she had a sweet sixteen birthday party at her dads pub. Of course, I was invited.

Irene lived on the far side of Wigan in a very depressed area. But because the party might last well into the night and the last bus out of Wigan for Orrell was eleven o'clock she asked me if I would care to stay over at her house.

At her party Irene met John Cartwright, a frequent patron of the pub, a young lad of seventeen.

In those day our lives were basically centered around the pubs, they were the neighborhood gathering place, you could buy pub meals and a pint and there were, more often than not kids there with their parents.

Nobody cared about I.D's, a pint of beer, well just about everybody drank beer.

The party was a great success and we all had lots of fun.

As the party was winding down, Irene was nowhere to be found, and John Cartwright was also missing.

Irene had two sisters. The oldest, Elsie was mentally retarded. Then came Marjory, who was of normal stature and seemed to tower over the rest of her family. Irene was the youngest.

Irene's dad closed the pub at 2:00 am and still no Irene. I walked to their house with the rest of the family.

I was made very welcome. We all had a cup of tea and sat around and talked for a while until

Irene finally came home. She was all aglow and proclaiming she now had a new boyfriend.

The house, with its swayed back roof had two tiny bedrooms upstairs and I wondered where I was supposed to sleep. I soon found out.

In the tiny upstairs back bedroom was one double bed. Elsie and Marjory slept with their heads at the top of the bed and Irene and I slept with our heads at the foot of the bed. I had two pairs of legs on either side of me.

Irene apologized for the cramped sleeping arrangements saying that usually she was the only one who slept at the bottom of the bed, so it wasn't usually so crowded.

In the weeks that followed we would run into John Cartwright once in a while when we went to her dad's pub for a pint. He wasn't the most attentive of boyfriends.

About a couple of months later, it became obvious that Irene was pregnant. She was terrified of telling her dad.

But it could not be kept quiet for long and John Cartwright and Little Irene were basically forced, by the traditions of society, to get married.

The next party I attended at the pub was a wedding party.

Irene's life was now changed forever.

I didn't see her much over the next few months; our lives had gone in completely different directions.

Then after the baby was born, a little girl, who she named Angela, I found out where she lived and went to visit.

Terraced housing

The little terraced house where she now lived, if possible, was smaller and in worse condition than the one she had grown up in. It was a couple of streets over from her parents.

The house, whose front door opened directly onto the street was a dismal affair.

The interior was dark and sparsely furnished. Irene was sitting on a broken down, threadbare couch, in front of a dimly lit coal fire, which did little to take the chill out of the room.

A single lightbulb hung from the ceiling the only light in the dim interior.

The baby Angela was asleep in her pram. Irene said she was going to get a cot as soon as they could afford one.

I asked if John was home. "No not yet," she said, "he general goes over to the pub after work and probably won't be home 'till late."

She offered me a cup of tea which I accepted, and we sat together far into the evening. Still no John.

She told me she was alone most days, and that John came home drunk most every night, staying awake just long enough to knock her around a bit then stumble off to bed and the next day do it all over again. He spent most of his wages at the pub and there was little left for food and essentials.

This was the most depressing thing I had ever witnessed, and I had witnessed a lot for my young age.

She cried when I left. She was so unhappy.

As I left that evening to catch the bus for home, I felt so disheartened. Is this it? Could that have been me? Was that what I had to look forward to? Marrying a local lad, raising a bunch of kids, growing old before my time, while he spent his nights down at the pub?

The next day after work, I went into the Army recruiting office with the intention of joining up. I just knew I had to get out of Wigan, by any means possible.

But I was either the luckiest person alive or the most unlucky, whichever way you choose to view it because they told me to come back when I was seventeen.

39

CANADA

While my life was following its dismal path, things at home were taking a turn for the worse.

The running of the manufacturing part of the shoe factory was in my Dad's hands and was running like a well-oiled machine. Bill Brown was holding up the financial end.

But Bill Brown was not the stalwart friend my Dad thought he was and in a little less than a year, he had absconded with all the remaining funds after embezzling everything else, never to be seen again.

Suddenly everything dried up. The factory closed and my parents were stuck with having to figure out how they were going to pay the mortgage on the new house.

My Mother and Dad being very adaptable people, opened up a small shop in Wigan and started selling secondhand goods.

Meanwhile across the country, in the county of Yorkshire, the Bennet family were having struggles of their own.

The long years of horror in the German prisoner of war camp had taken a dreadful toll on my Uncle Ernie and coupled with the fact that the war had plunged the country into an economic crisis, he was unable to find work.

Work was scarce even for those men in good health.

Uncle Ernie approached my Dad with the idea of both families leaving England in pursuit of a new and better life in Canada where it was considered as having countless opportunities.

With our family's future looking grim, my Dad agreed.

Uncle Ernie would lead the charge by going over first to get established then we all would follow.

Uncle Ernie sold their house and Auntie Dilla and their two children Susan and Andrew would come and stay with us in the meantime.

They contacted their American brother-in-law my Uncle John Maples and he agreed to go up to Canada to help get Ernie established.

But the trip proved a disaster.

In today's climate it would have been obvious that Ernie Bennett was suffering from severe Post-Traumatic Stress Disorder.

Since coming home from the war, he had never been far from his wife, children or his home. But he thought that getting away and starting a new life would be the answer.

But he found when he got to Canada, he could not cope, fear incapacitated him and he froze. He found himself incapable of even leaving his hotel room even with the help of John Maples.

Uncle John tried every means possible to snap Uncle Ernie out of his fears to no avail and after just a short time informed my Dad that the only thing to do was for Ernie to come back home.

But Uncle Ernie had no home to come back to and had to depend on the charity of others to survive. I cannot imagine his desolation and the feelings of failure he must have gone through.

Uncle Ernie moved back to England to stay with us; he was in complete depression.

While Uncle Ernie had been in Canada the atmosphere at #39 Hayes Rd had become very strained.

I suppose, for my parents and Auntie Dilla, this was an extremely stressful time also. Their futures were rocky at best and as things deteriorated in Canada, they became even rockier. Probably made worse by the fact that two households were trying to coexist under one roof.

My Mother was not a very flexible person to start with, even with her own sister. My Dad stayed detached.

And to make matters worse, there were us three sisters on the one side and a brother and sister, our cousins on the other that were practically strangers.

Susan and Andrew Bennett had been raised far differently than we three.

They had been raised by a loving mother, lived close to relatives, and had not been exposed to as much trauma from the war that had been laid out our feet.

Uncle Ernie never talked about his time as a prisoner of war, so how much they knew of their fathers' experiences as a prisoner I do not know.

They were both of a quieter nature and spoke and acted very reserved. A far cry from the three of us who had basically raised ourselves and were more than a little rough around the edges.

I don't seem to have much recall of that time but according to Laura we were far from welcoming.

Andrew, two years younger than Stella was a quiet, pale boy who had no interest in playing outside, and we thought of him as a sissy.

Cousin Susan, two years younger than me was also completely alien to us, soft spoken, quiet, and of a very gentle nature. She always wore a dress and never wanted to get herself dirty.

My mother had very little patience with either of them, and Susan later recalled that she was terrified of my Mother who did nothing to stop the bullying that evidently us three inflicted on the two of them.

Susan, if you ever read this book, I am so terribly sorry for whatever I put you through.

40

ANTIQUES

In the early eighteen hundred's, Northern England had marched proudly into the industrial revolution and experienced dramatic economic expansion and a rapid rise in the population.

Wigan became known as a major cotton mill and coal mining town.

By the early 1900s, coal mining was at its peak, and there were at least a thousand mine shafts within five miles of the town center.

As the town had grown, the majority of Wigan's population were laborers and they needed housing. So, row after row of low-income terraced housing had sprung up to accommodate them.

As the years went by these areas deteriorated and soon parts of Wigan became a very depressed slum area.

But the post-war years were a period of **great change in the working lives of many Britons.**

Industry was changing and the needs of the local people were changing too. It was a time for expansion and modernization of the downtown and surrounding area.

Many new businesses were moving in, department stores, supermarkets. And with them came more automobiles and then the need for parking structures and wider roads.

With the local economy on the rise, people found their wages growing too and so the building trade flourished as new developments emerged and more and more families moved to the suburbs.

Slowly the skyline of Wigan started to change, in place of the row upon row of decrepit terraced houses, modern, low-income flats rose up everywhere, some many stories high.

And although this was a great time of growth for Wigan it was a traumatic time for the many elderly and very poor who had lived in the terraced houses all their lives.

Suddenly they were told they had to move. Some would move in with family members or be put in an *'old folks'* home, and many who had nowhere else to go were relocated to one of the many new flats.

Many of the elderly whose families had lived in the same house for several generation were sitting on priceless antiques.

Some pieces bought for pennies years ago were now worth much more. Some were family heirlooms that had been sitting on a mantle or stashed away in an attic. Or they had been brought to England by soldiers fighting in foreign wars as souvenirs.

Suddenly antiques started flooding the market. Auction houses became overflowing with priceless antiques. And my parents saw a great opportunity.

If you were going to get into the antique business, the 1950's was the time to do it.

My Mother put her keen mind to work and soon learned to identify a good piece and became very adept at dating items.

And not only the English but Americans too greatly desired these antiques. And business boomed.

A new practice in the antique business emerged; it was called house clearing.

A family, having to place their elderly relatives in one of the new flats, sold off a house's contents for one lump sum and with the money were able to buy some more modern, less bulky furniture for their loved ones.

An antique dealer would be called in to look around and give the homeowner or their relative a flat fee for everything.

Many unsuspecting people became victims of this practice as unscrupulous dealers were not going to give a better price when a good piece was found up in an attic or down in a basement.

But my Dad had a lot of integrity and when he found an item that was of value, he would tell the homeowner and give them a fair market price.

My Dads reputation grew as a fair and honest man and word spread and soon people were waiting until he was available to buy their houses contents rather than bring in a less know dealer.

I remember my parents often coming back from an auction or a house clearing with wonderful works of art.

One piece in particular stands out in my mind. They came into the living room carrying and placing on the dining room table a huge blown glass galleon. It was so large it covered the top of the table.

The masts and ropes were made from thin threads of glass, an absolute work of art and how it had survived through the years is beyond me.

41

TEENAGERS

For us three girl's life continued on its merry path.

Stella was still in school; Laura was working in a department store and I was jumping from one meaningless job to another.

But we were teenagers and it takes a lot to keep a sixteen-year-old down for long. Yes, the desire to move away from Wigan never left me.

Even though I did try to live life to its fullest.

We all worked Monday through Friday and on payday the bulk of our pay went to our parents.

We got to keep a small percentage, which we called pocket money and after all the bus fares and entertainment, there was not much left.

Friday night and the weekends were a time for fun.

We would go to the pubs on Friday nights, and believe me there were plenty of them. I think Wigan has a pub on every street corner. This was a great time and place for socializing.

Romances began and romances ended on Fridays. There was always someone with a broken heart and someone who had just fallen hopelessly in love.

For those of us who lived in one of the suburbs, like we did, night came to a screeching halt about 10:45 pm as we made a mad dash to the town center where the last bus left at 11:00 o'clock sharp. If you missed the last bus it meant a long walk home.

Our parents didn't question what time we got home; the only stipulation was that when we did get home we came in quietly so as not to wake them.

Although later in life my Dad did tell me that he would lay awake waiting for the last one of us to return home.

He said he used to say to himself after we were all home, "All's in that matters."

Most Saturday afternoons we would once again venture into Wigan and shop the markets and department stores and the sidewalks would be teeming with pedestrians.

Saturday afternoon in downtown Wigan 1960's

No shopping malls in those days.

Then, more often than not we would go to a local café for a cup of tea and go over the day's purchases.

Saturday night was date night.

Now nobody had cars back then, so arrangements were made to meet at the town center where a double decker bus came by every few minutes.

Bus depot in town centre 1950s

The double decker bus was everyone's means of transportation. You could go anywhere and everywhere by bus.

On a date we would usually go for a pub dinner, then on to the Pictures (*movies*) were we would hold hands and neck. And the back row would be filled with our friends doing the same thing.

Sunday's everything was closed, except for private clubs and the pubs had limited hours.

If the weather was nice, we would go to Wigan Park, a public park in the middle of town. It has wonderful formal gardens surrounded by green lawns, children's playgrounds, mini golf, sports grounds and a café, and covered about fourteen acres.

Or we would walk the trails of Haigh Hall, this was a grand country house that had been bought by the town of Wigan in 1947 and the grounds were opened to the public.

The house, which is an historic site was built in the mid-19th century within a landscaped park occupying about one hundred acres. The site is now a public park with walled gardens and woodland pathways.

Now if the weather was permitting like in July and August when we could expect a few weeks of sunny skies and temperatures in the mid to upper 70's, we would hop a train and go to the open-air baths in Southport or to the beach at Blackpool.

With Blackpool Tower rising over the city, a carbon copy, although not as famous, as the Eiffel Tower in Paris.

Blackpool was lots of fun. It had three long piers stretching out over the sea and board walks along the beach with cafes, pubs and carnival rides for the kids. And the sidewalks would be packed with holiday makers and of course groups of young men there for us to flirt with.

Then stopping into a pub for a pint and plate of fish and chips.

Once a year Blackpool would have a light festival called Blackpool Illuminations, and the whole sea front would be ablaze with a thousand lights.

But life was not all fun and games. Monday morning, we were all back to reality.

Since I was not qualified for anything meaningful, my only options were menial jobs with little pay and no future.

I would soon be eighteen and nothing to show for it.

Canada, Australia, New Zealand and West Africa were a part of the British Commonwealth and English citizens could immigrate to any of these countries. All you needed was to be eighteen to travel there alone, some travelling money and the willingness to take a chance. Well one out of three wasn't bad. I had the willingness; next I needed some travelling money,

I realize now that this was all a fool's dream, but if you don't have a dream you can't have a dream come true, right?

I heard they were hiring and paying well at the Trencherfield Cotton Mill.

Now the most depressing, most hard labor intense and most dangerous job in England was to be a miner in the numerous coal pits in Northern England. If you worked at the mine, you were considered to be on the lowest rung of the ladder.

The next step up was the cotton mill.

I think this was the most awful and unbearable job I had while still in England.

The Trencherfield Cotton Mill stood next to the Leeds and Liverpool Canal in downtown Wigan so the cotton could be loaded onto barges for transportation to the docks at Liverpool.

Trencherfield Cotton Mill

On my first day it was like stepping back in to the early 1900's.

It had not changed much since it was built in 1907 and was still driven by the same 2,500 hp engine that turned a huge fly wheel at breakneck speed, which ran all the machinery.

The working conditions in the mill were notoriously bad, not to mention dangerous.

Some mills in the county had been updated but the Trencherfield had not.

There were many dangers that mill workers were exposed to on a daily basis.

There were no safety guards on the large machines and accidents were commonplace.

The spinning rooms were the worse, hot and humid. This was to prevent the thread from breaking and the air was thick with cotton fluff, especially in the carding rooms that would burn my eyes and throat.

I was overwhelmed by the noise the machinery made and the speed with which the huge machines crashed back and forth, but I persevered.

42

BEAT PENNI

Just up the street from us on Hayes Road lived a girl named Beatrice Pennington but we all called Beat Penni for short. She was three years older than I and a year older than my sister Laura.

We all ran around in the same crowd and she and I soon became friends in spite of our age difference. I was seventeen and she was twenty-one.

We all often went on the train to Manchester where the night life was booming especially around the Manchester University area were students from all over the world converged.

On one of these trips my sister Laura met a Turkish university student name Edip, a man she would eventually marry.

At first my parents were against the relationship between Laura and Edip, not because they were prejudiced, far from it. But they knew he would, when his studies were over, return to Turkey and they understood the drastic difference in the culture of life should Laura go back there with him. But Laura would not be deterred.

After they married, she would spend the next fifteen years in the exotic and alien world of the Turkish empire.

Beat Penni had a Grammar school and college education and was the corporate secretary to the General Manager of Heinz Foods.

Heinz Foods had two plants in the Wigan area, one, a new plant in Kitt Green, a small suburb of Wigan and the original plant located on the other side of Wigan in Standish. The home and named for the famous Miles Standish.

When Beatrice realized I was working at the Trencherfield cotton mill, she was appalled and offered to talk to her boss and see if she could exert any influence and get me a job.

Heinz Foods, was a modern plant that paid exceptionally well and had a waiting list of perspective employees, but Beatrice was able to get me hired on at the Standish plant.

The Kit Green plant was just a short bus ride from Hayes road, but the Standish plant, unfortunately, would mean an arduous trip back and forth to work each day, but I didn't mind.

A ten-minute walk to the bus stop, a twenty-minute bus ride into Wigan, changing buses in Wigan town center, then a fifteen-minute bus ride to Standish and another ten-minute walk to the plant.

I was hired on in 1961.

Even though this was still factory work they paid extremely well, and the working conditions were a far cry from the Trencherfield Cotton mill, and I worked every chance I got to feather my nest for my get-away from Wigan.

While working there I met Alan Norris. He was my second love.

But it wasn't long before the wanderlust struck me again and again, and I wanted to be off to parts unknown.

But then wonderful news. My Mother, writing to her sister, my Aunt Lucy mentioned my obsession to leave England.

Aunt Lucy suggested I come to America.

My big chance had come at last.

I had never told Alan of my desire to leave but the relationship didn't seem to be going anywhere. He never seemed to want to take it to the next level. He was quite content with the way things were.

After I told him the news, he just walked away. I did not see him again until the day before I was due to sail. He came to my house and asked me to marry him. But by then it was too late.

43

AMERICA

When my day for departure arrived, I could hardly contain my excitement.

But for the rest of the family it was just another damp and foggy day. Just another wrinkle in the fabric of ordinary life.

On a chilly day in April 1962, I left England behind. I was going to America; my big day had come at last.

I sailed out of Liverpool.

My parents, sister Laura and best friend Beat Penni came to see me off.

When we arrived at the Liverpool docks, the damp gray fog hid the huge black ship in its midst and it wasn't until the mid-morning winds chased away the gray clouds that I finally got a look at that great vessel that was to take me to my future.

Finally, the pale sun peeked through and was full of warmth. It shimmered off the oily black water of Liverpool Harbor, revealing a filthy collection of garbage and dead fish floating on the surface. Seagulls screamed in noisy circles overhead and squabbled over the spoils. Ships from all over the world sat at berth there; it was a busy port.

The sight of the sea and the warmth of the sun fired my senses with exhilaration, and I looked impatiently out across the heaving waters. The R.M.S. Sylvania, an ocean-going vessel of the Cunard line, sat proudly in her moorings; that great ship had been waiting for me all my life.

THE RMA SYLVANIA OF THE CUNARD LINE

In my heart there was a wonderful, joyous feeling. I had no regrets; I knew deep down I was making the right decision.

Laura hugged me goodbye and I felt uncomfortable but happy with her sadness.

My Dad, uncomfortable with any show of affection, just nodded his head in farewell, not quite sure what he should do.

I leaned over and hugged him and then he turned and walked away, and I wondered, even hoped, that he was shedding a tear.

I was glad that Stella and I had said our good-byes at the house. Stella alone would have cried. Dear Stella was never afraid to show her true feelings.

My goodbyes to Beatrice were loud and boisterous with lots of promises to come and visit. I have never seen her since, although we did find each other a few years ago on Facebook.

Then I boarded my ship.

One person was allowed to accompany me on board to see me off.

My Mother followed me up the gangplank.

Now we were alone on that great sweeping stairway. I thought I saw a tear. At last, a show of emotion! Dear God, how I hoped it was real. And I suddenly felt guilty for feeling so happy that I was leaving, so I dropped a shadow over my face and buried my dreams and excitement, fearing that they lay bare and naked on my face, that somehow, she would take offense at my eagerness.

But my Mother made it easy for me, no long speeches, no asked-for promises, just a quick goodbye and then she was gone.

I went over to the rail, looked down, and saw them standing on the docks. They seemed small and far away.

I looked up at the skyline of Liverpool. A pall of dirty poisonous smog hung in the air, obliterating the tops of the buildings.

The ship sounded a loud blast of farewell and slipped her moorings, moving silently away from the wharf, pulled by two tugboats that were dwarfed by her hugeness. A cheer went up from the crowd below.

Many people were leaning over the rails waving goodbye. Some, like me, were leaving for good and I could see the emotions on their faces.

Others were going home to America after perhaps a holiday or a visit with family. They were happy and carefree, and soon drifted away from the rail.

I remember the acrid smell of the tugboats, the dank smell of the River Mersey, the way the skyline of huge buildings moved slowly past, how the sun struck them and made the windows glitter.

As the ship moved silently away from the dock, a lone Scotsman in full regalia walked smartly to the end of the pier and struck a mournful tune on his bagpipes. Strains of *"Will Ye No Come Back Agin'?"* drifted across the water towards me and finally melted my heart.

I suddenly felt a sorrow grip my soul and felt the cold chill of the tears that for the first time coursed down my face.

I stayed glued to the rail, watching as my country faded slowly into the past, and I thought of the people I was leaving behind. They too were now a part of the past.

I turned and went to the opposite side and stared out to the open sea.

A bright full moon was rising, hovering low over the water, casting a bright yellow glow on the shimmering surface of the ocean, a moon river lighting a pathway to my future.

I stood alone on the deck of that great ship, the other passengers long since gone below deck. I leaned against the railing and watched as England slowly disappeared below the horizon. I was not to see her again for many years.

The sun set, and as night came creeping on, that large, full, buttery moon filled the sky, and I saw the surface of the ocean shimmering in its beam. I thought again of the friends and family I was leaving behind. Their lives would go on as before, mine would be changed forever.

As I recall, I was not sad, I felt no pain. There was no regret to fill my heart, only a great joy, a feeling of freedom, and the excitement of the unknown.

I felt like I was poised on the starting line of a great race and the gun was about to go off. I walked to the front of the ship and looked out over the heaving ocean visible in the moon's glow.

A white sheet of spray burst up from the bow and appeared suspended in mid-air. Then the spray cascaded forward, and then down, and finally receded back into itself. I too felt suspended on that great ocean, suspended between the past and the future.

44

A WORD FROM STELLA

My name is Stella and I am the youngest of the Rothwell sisters.

When my sister Gillian left for America it was a time of great change for me. Not only was I losing my sister Gillian, my sister Laura was marrying her Turkish boyfriend Edip and it was only a matter of time before she would leave for Turkey, and also, we were losing our home.

Gillian leaving for America was a surreal event, something I could not, at first, wrap my mind around,

On the day she sailed Mum said I had to go to school, it was like. I was going to school and Gillian was going to America. Just like any normal day, life goes on, right.

It would be several weeks before the impact of her leaving really hit me.

Gillian and I had been close, we had been through a lot together. I suppose because I was closer in age to her than Laura. Laura was grown up; I was still considered a child.

My sisters had been my protectors all my life, now I was losing them both.

I remember how Gillian had looked after me when we had been sent to that horrendous Methodist school.

Suddenly I was going to be on my own.

After the collapse of our father's shoe factory and the failure of our emigration to Canada, the Rothwell's and the Bennett's were in a downhill spiral.

My Mum, Dad and Auntie Dilla had been selling secondhand goods in a small shop in Wigan, but it was not enough to pay the bills.

With the return of Uncle Ernie and my Dad's inability to pay the mortgage on Hayes Rd, drastic and immediate changes had to be made.

Hayes road and the secondhand shop were sold and the Bennet family moved to Ince, a suburb of Wigan and started their own second hand shop.

My Dad and Mum bought a small shop with living quarters located on Wigan Lane.

When we moved into Wigan Lane, it was a total disaster. The place was literally falling to pieces.

There was no bathroom, just a small toilet and two upstairs rooms. On the first floor, behind the shop, was a small living area, and behind that a lean-to with a small kitchen sink. The roof was leaking so bad that if it was raining when we washed dishes, we had to use an umbrella. Everywhere there were leaks and on a rainy day you could hear the water dripping into pans all over the upstairs rooms,

But my Mum and Dad plodded on undaunted and with the help of Uncle Ernie, working day and night, soon made it all livable. I really have to give them their due; they were very hard workers.

The shop at one time had been a Butchers Shop and more recently a Bakery that sold bread out of the store front and when they left, unfortunately, they did not take their rats with them who had set up house in the attic and at night when all was quiet we could hear them scurrying about in the ceiling. I thought it was the end of the world.

Since I was in my final year of school, rather than start a new school in Wigan I stayed on at St James Secondary Modern and rode the local bus back and forth making the long bus ride to and from school every day. Although I must admit after we made the move to Wigan Lane, I missed more days than I attended, but since it was just a Secondary Modern School, nobody seemed to care anyway.

I lived on Wigan Lane until my marriage in 1967.

Laura had married her Turkish boyfriend Edip and they had a son, but even though they spent some of their time in Manchester near the University, they spent most of their time on Wigan Lane.

Laura, Edip and the baby had the back bedroom. I shared the front room with Mum and Dad, sleeping on a mattress on the floor.

Edip had almost finished his studies at the Manchester University and soon they would be moving to Turkey, then I would be able to have my own room.

We all did what we could to improve our living conditions and before long. it really started to take shape. The rats were gone from the attic and the roof had been repaired.

My parents had come a long way in a short time to make the little shop a home.

Auntie Dilla and Uncle Ernie did not have the business ability to make their secondhand shop work, so Uncle Ernie went to work in the building trade, which was booming at that time, as a bricklayer and was a bricklayer for the rest of his working life, earning enough money for them to live a comfortable life.

Mum and Dad soon set their sights on antiques rather than secondhand goods, and this proved to be their strength.

With my Dad's good business sense and my Mums ability to realize a good and genuine antique from a fake, their business soon took off and before you know it, we were back in the money again.

I must say, after all is said and done, the Wigan Lane shop was a place we could be proud of. It was clean, quaint and very comfortable. And my Mum and Dad seemed to be happy again. After I married and moved out, Mum and Dad made the back-upstairs room their bedroom and the front bedroom a formal sitting room. The little front bedroom window was replaced by a large picture window that look down on busy Wigan Lane.

Our lives have been a roller coaster of ups and downs, but we have all come out on top. I think all three of us sisters inherited the strength, ability and stoic nature of our parents that helped us make it through, against all odds, the most trying of times as our parents had done.

Stella Rothwell Rendowski

45

A VISIT TO WIGAN

I could not finish this book without telling of my parents' success.

My first visit back to England, after many years in America, was a very emotional time. I think more so for me than anyone else.

All of our lives had gone down completely different paths and even though we were family we were also strangers.

My Dad, still loving but quiet and unemotional, my Mother distant and a little put out by the disruption my visit caused her.

When I arrived at the shop on Wigan Lane, I walked into the most thriving and interesting of antique shops.

The Wigan lane shop in the 1800's

The façade of the building had been transformed and now sported a wide store window with a large sign above it proclaiming the treasures inside.

ROTHWELL'S ANTIQUES

Telephone: WIGAN 45467

G. Rothwell

77 WIGAN LANE
WIGAN

Antiques
Bought & sold

Above, on the second floor and just as large, was a big picture window that overlooked the hustle and bustle of busy Wigan Lane.

This building, that was over two hundred years old, was now in tip top condition and the perfect setting for the treasures within.

The shops interior, bright and airy was cluttered with priceless antique's and the glass display counter gleamed with rings, broaches and pocket watches, shining in gold and silver.

Through a door into the living area, it was even more magnificent. You walked on Persian rugs and could hear the ticking of several grandfather clocks, each a treasure in its own right.

Bronzes, Alabaster figures, Cloisonné plagues, a Ming vase stood in the corner.

A multiple drawer display cabinet with my Dads collection of pocket watches, priceless. Valuable paintings were on the walls. Too much for my eyes to take in. This was their retirement.

A modern kitchen with modern appliances seemed out of place in the splendor of all these ancient treasures.

In the dining area we ate our meals on fine china and drank from crystal cut glasses and sat on Queen Anne chairs at a table covered with a Damask tablecloth.

Out back was a small walled in garden. One wall was completely covered in purple Clematis, and a multitude of flowers in every color imaginable was tucked into every available corner.

As you climbed the stairs, you could hear the creak of old worn boards on the steps beneath your feet.

At the top of the stairs, a small but modern bathroom, and the back room a light airy bedroom.

The front living room, with the large picture window overlooking Wigan Lane, lit up the interior of this beautiful room, even more splendid than the downstairs, antiques everywhere. A priceless sword collection taking up one whole wall.

You can see some of the swords reflected in the mirror

The visit, after my years absent, was wonderful, walking again on the streets of my youth and tasting the food I had grown up on. Bangers and mash, meat and potato pie, lamb chops and roasted potatoes. A visit to the fish and chip shop and a pub lunch and a pint at The Brocket Arms.

Spending time with my sisters. Having a laugh, exchanging stories and reminiscing about the past.

A trip back to Farington to # 1 Glouster Ave., still standing after all these years and the house in Orrell where I spent my teen years. My old alma mater, St James Secondary Modern School. The Trencherfield Cotton Mill. Wigan Pier and walks down the Liverpool Leeds canal. A stroll through Haig Hall with its towering Rhododendron's dripping with flowers.

Before I finish, I must tell you of an incident that occurred during that first visit to the little Antique shop on Wigan Lane.

My Mother was a very intelligent, attractive woman and I have the utmost respect for her. But having said that, none of us ever had that mother and daughter relationship with her that most kids enjoy. It's hard to explain but she was more just like a person we just happened to know.

Now whether a curse or a blessing, she also had a sixth sense; it was something that we grew up with, it was just a part of our lives and it became more obvious the older she got and manifested itself even more when they got into the antique trade where she was surrounded by numerous items from the distant past.

Some good antique buys she would pass up because she claimed she got very bad vibes from, and according to my Dad, many houses, slated for a house clearing, she avoided like the plague.

Since they only had one bedroom, when I came to visit, they got an inflatable mattress and I slept on the floor in the living room upstairs. Around two a.m., on that first night, when we were all in bed, I was awakened by the boards creaking on the stairsteps. I assumed one of my parents had gone downstairs for something and thought nothing of it. The next morning, I made the comment on how much louder the creaking on the stairs was during the quietness of the night. My Mother nonchalantly explained to me that the spirit of a young woman climbed the stairs every evening about the same time and not to worry. Yes, I don't blame you; I was sceptic too.

The next night I decided to check it out for myself and waited, laying there in the dark for the telltale creaking on the stairs.

I had no idea of the time because when I had first arrived my Dad had stopped all his many clocks because he thought that the constant ticking and the hourly striking would keep me awake.

As the minutes dragged on, my impatience mounted, although I wasn't sure what I was planning to do if I was confronted by a ghost, but I felt the need to find out.

When I heard the creaking on the stairs again, my heart jumped, and I sprang to my feet and went out onto the landing to investigate.

A blast of cold air hit me as I opened the door and I felt my nerve deserting me. I looked quickly over the railing to the stairs below, but all was dark and quiet. I am not sure whether I was disappointed or relieved.

As I turned to go back to bed, I let out a gasp of surprise when I saw my Mother standing there on the landing.

"Gilly, what on earth are you doing?"

"Eh, I thought I heard a noise," I answered

"It's probably just the old house settling in for the night," she said, turning around and going back into her room, closing the door behind her.

A decided chill ran down my spine. Then I heard the distinct sound of a clock striking the two-a.m. hour. Surely my Dad must have forgotten to stop one of the clocks downstairs. I hurried to my bed, closing the door behind me. That was enough excitement for one night.

The next morning, I asked my parents about the event I had experienced, and they told me that they have had many such occurrences over the years and not to worry. Easier said than done! And yes, my Dad said, all the clocks were stopped.

I still, to this day cannot find any reasonable explanation for what I experienced.

A few items from my Parents Portfolio

P.J. MENE: BRONZE HORSE, "IBRAHIM",

French Bronze1780    *Alabaster figurine 1851*

Reclining Bronze 'Aphrodite' 1880

Japanese Vase 1700's

Chinese Vase 1850

Cloisonné Plate 1880

Wedgewood Plate

(A view of the upstairs sitting room)

Grandfather clock 1700's. German Movement

Cossack with Maiden 1831
Russian Bronze (one of my Dads favorite pieces)

My sisters and I, like our parents are the epitome of survival and endurance.

Through sheer determination we have all survived the ups and downs of circumstances, some of our own making, some that were beyond our control.

My parents lived quite comfortable through their aging years, visiting Turkey to see Laura and also spending several summers with me in America. But the modernization of Wigan soon meant the final days for the little shop on Wigan Lane and it too is now just a memory.

My parents spent their final years in a wonderful old house in the town of Wigan.

In loving memory

George and Grace Elizabeth Rothwell

Words of wisdom from my Dad.

You can follow the trek of your life by the good times and the bad times. If there weren't any bad times you would have nothing to compare the good times with.

Words of wisdom from my Mother

If you cannot change something, instead of learning to accept it, put your boxing gloves on and fight like hell until you do. Do not go quietly into that dark night.

Words from me.

If I could go back in time, I would tell my teachers and my younger self that I was not a failure. That I would get out of Wigan, be happy and successful. Even write a book, heck, write two books.

Made in the USA
Columbia, SC
04 March 2020